# Born to
# Be Wild

### Book 4

### Born Series

## Susan Horsnell

## USA Today Bestselling Author

Contents:

BORN TO BE WILD

Copyright © 2021 by Susan Horsnell

Written by Susan Horsnell

Edit: Redline Editing

Line Edit by Robyn Corcoran

Proofread by Leanne Rogers.

**Warning:**

This book contains sexual content, a m/m scene and language suitable only for those 18+ If you have enjoyed this book, please take the time to leave a review.

Thank you.

THANKS

Thank you to Blake Sevani who willingly answered my questions on strength training

# Prologue

*Present Day*

**LIAM**

The lights of the club dimmed. A spotlight appeared over center stage and a voice boomed over the loudspeakers.

"And, now please welcome the main attraction of the *Velvet Post*. Our very own Devil in disguise – Lee!"

Chatter ceased. Not a sound filtered through from the main area of the club where I waited beneath the stage. You could have heard a pin drop.

I gripped the pole, propelled myself almost to the top and wrapped one leg securely around the shimmering post, resting my other booted foot against my knee.

"Ready?" Pedro asked.

I nodded. Music thundered as the platform I was on began to rise. I didn't need to glance up to know thick smoke billowed above me. I would emerge from it like I had done every night for the past three years.

I waited until my torso had cleared the floor of the stage and pressed a small button on the edge of my wings. The enormous wings eased open and scattered red lights flashed amongst the black feathers. The platform continued to rise and gripping the pole with my right arm and foot, I stretched out my left leg and arm until I was in a spread-eagled position. The smoke thinned and wafted away as the platform clicked and locked into place at stage level.

Men whistled and surged forward as I twisted erotically and slowly slid from the pole. The club was packed; I would make good money tonight.

***

**STEVE**

I stood with my eyes riveted on the figure on stage. Shady was right; the main attraction at the *Velvet Post* – a gay strip club, was indeed my brother.

Liam had walked away - actually he'd run from our family four years ago. It was after he'd helped cause the death of Keegan's baby and almost Keegan herself. He was just shy of seventeen at the time and had seemingly disappeared into thin air. It took seven months for a private detective to eventually track him down in a seedy part of Linton.

I'd gone down and talked with him; tried to get him to come home but he'd refused. Liam was convinced we all hated him and he'd argued that he needed to stay away so he couldn't ruin our lives more than he already had. He said he'd come back when he felt the time was right and not before. None of us were happy about his decision but we left him be. What else could we do?

Another five months passed and there was still no sign that Liam would come home. Once a month, Mom would receive a letter telling her he was happy and taking care of himself. It was never postmarked and always hand delivered, which I found strange.

Mom shed rivers of tears for her first born - I'm the eldest but was adopted when I was seven years old. When she couldn't wait any longer for my brother to make the decision to return home, she insisted I tell her where he was living and reluctantly I gave her his address. Mom rushed down to talk with him but he was gone. He'd left the Chinese restaurant, where he'd been working, a week after I'd been to see him and seemingly vanished into thin air. Again. Mrs. Chin, the owner, had no idea where he'd gone and like my mother, she was heartbroken. Mom promised to let her know if we heard anything from him.

Mom insisted on hiring the private detective again to bring him back home, but Dad said it would be a waste of the man's time. Even if they could force my brother to return home, the minute they turned their backs, he'd be gone again. He said Liam had to want to come back on his own.

Mom argued but she knew Dad was right. So, even though it broke her heart, she left my brother alone. She said if the notes stopped or, he didn't see her within ten years, she was going to find him and talk with him, no matter what. Dad agreed that was fair enough.

I put word out on the streets the following day, I needed to know where he was for my own peace of mind. Even if I didn't contact him; I would at least know how to in the case of an emergency.

When my wife, Keegan, was pregnant with our first born - Natasha Elizabeth, I'd desperately wanted to tell him. I wanted him to know his niece and watch her grow up, be an important part of her life. To do what uncles did with their nieces and nephews. Despite all my efforts, he couldn't be found and I'd learnt to deal with not knowing where he was.

When Keegan fell pregnant again, my determination to find him surfaced again. I put word out in the neighborhood where I had a business as a Social Worker. I contacted questionable characters who seemed to know the ins and outs of the streets and begged for their help, convincing Mom and Dad, it would be better than re-hiring the private investigator who wasn't familiar with the 'hood part of town.

I was well liked in the poorest parts of town because I did a lot to help those who felt trapped in dire situations; I gave people hope. So, when word got out *I* needed help to search for my brother, people from all over turned up on my doorstep.

My partner, Jeremy and I were kept busy handing out photos and answering questions. It gave me hope we would find him, but days turned to weeks with nothing, not even a hint. Again, he'd eluded us. It was if he'd dropped off the planet. I'd even begun to fear he might be dead after remembering where he'd first lived.

Keegan and I welcomed Alexander Liam into our family with everyone but his Uncle Liam for whom he was named. It was breaking my heart.

Then, earlier this evening, exactly four years after Liam had left home, two days before his twenty-first birthday, Shady Fitzroy turned up at our office. I was in the process of locking up.

*** 

"Steve, I think I've found your brother. Got a minute to talk?"

Shady was one of the more questionable characters I'd ask to search for Liam. I knew he indulged in illegal activities but as long as they didn't involve me, or anyone I looked after, I left him be. It was none of my business how he made his money. I unlocked the office and seconds later we were seated in the reception area. Every nerve in my body danced with excitement.

"Where?"

Shady leaned back in the chair and thrust Liam's picture at me. "He don't look much like that now."

"I knew he wouldn't. That was taken when he was barely seventeen, four years ago. It was the last one before he left."

"His hair is jet black now and a bit longer. He's around the same height as you and has got the body of a god. He's a dancer and goes by the name – Lee."

Lee – the name Mom always called him. "A dancer?" My hopes were dashed yet again. It couldn't be him. My brother couldn't dance to save his life. "How do you know it's him?"

"I don't for sure, but there's no mistaking his eyes and the shape of his face. He wears a mask but you can see enough to know it's him."

"So, you're telling me, you think it's him because of his eyes and the shape of his face."

"Not only that. He's the image of your dad - Hamish."

Tingles danced up and down my spine. Shady had known my dad from when they'd both lived here more than twenty years ago. Liam had resembled Dad all his life.

"Where's the club and what's the name?"

"Central Downtown. The *Velvet Post.*"

"The *Velvet Post*? That's a ......"

"Gay strip club," Shady finished.

"He's a stripper in a gay club in Nollet? How the fuck did he end up there?"

"*Lee* is the main attraction and fucking good. He must be making a fortune judging by the amount of money I saw being shoved into his G-string and thrown onto the stage last night. He does one show at 8pm dressed as a Devil and one at 11pm dressed as an Angel. The men go wild for him."

13

I groaned. "How will I explain this to Mom? Fuck, how will I explain it to Dad?" I swallowed hard and locked my eyes on Shady. "Is he gay? Does he get paid to let other men fuck him?"

"Dunno, but being the betting man I am, I'd put my next pay packet on him batting for the other team. Straight men don't dance for a club full of gay men. I knew you'd be concerned about him being a whore so I asked around. The dancers there don't fuck the clientele but they do give private lap dances. Lee, however, doesn't even do that. He makes plenty from dancing I reckon."

I nodded. Liam being gay didn't matter of course. Hell, Uncle Wade and Uncle Rafe were gay and we loved them dearly. I was privileged to have them as my Godfathers. Dad even had a weekend of gay sex with Uncle Wade before he met Mom. It taught him how to love, not only those around him but also himself. I was relieved to know my brother didn't whore himself out.

I would never have picked Liam for being gay when we were growing up. He was always in trouble for cornering girls and sneaking a kiss. A gay strip club was the last place I would have thought to look for him. I wondered if confusion about his sexual preference could have been the cause of his anger and moodiness. Was he having difficulty coming to terms with the fact he was gay? Didn't he know he could talk to us; it would have made no difference to those of us who loved him? I was puzzled as to why he hadn't discussed it with our uncles but I'd ask him about that once I saw him.

Deep in thought, I'd forgotten about Shady until he spoke. "What are you gonna do?"

"Eight is his first show?"

"Yep and believe me, you want to see it. Word on the street about him was right. His Angel is great but the Devil is fucking dynamite. Every cock in the place, including mine, was as hard as the pole he was dancing around. Your brother is so fucking sexy. Hell, I found myself wanting to be gay while I watched his cute ass and his huge package jiggling around."

I growled at Shady's words, stood and offered him a few bills from my wallet which he quickly accepted and spirited away into his pocket. "Thanks for the info. I'll go tonight."

I walked the man out and locked up again. I had just enough time to go home, change and make it to the club for the eight o'clock show.

My heartbeat spiked at the thought that I was finally going to speak to my brother after more than three years of silence.

***

My focus returned to my brother as he strutted to the edge of the stage. He wore knee length black boots and huge black wings rose from his back. A mask covered his eyes but even from where I stood, I could see they were the vivid green he'd been born with. There was no doubt this man was my brother. Red lights flashed around him and accentuated the fiery red of his sparkling G-string. He was taller than when I'd spoken to him three years ago and he'd filled out. His chest was broad, every muscle well defined.

He lowered to the floor with his knees spread wide apart. Men pushed and shoved forward in an effort to jam cash into his G-string. No doubt even more eager for a feel of my brother's obviously huge cock. His hips gyrated. His G-string bulged with cash.

He stood and danced back to the middle of the stage, leapt onto the pole and performed some astonishing tricks. The men's initial groans of disappointment when he'd strutted away, turned to wolf whistling and catcalling as we all got a great view of his firm, naked ass.

The leaps and pirouettes he performed were equal to those performed by dancers in the New York ballet. I had to admit, Liam was both beautiful and talented. I felt proud of him and his performance. His wings opened and closed as he spun on the pole. Gyrating, legs up, legs down.

When he hung upside down, his head near the floor and his legs in the splits along the pole; even I clapped enthusiastically. He was as supple as a piece of elastic.

I wondered how he'd ended up in a place like this. Highbrow, yes, but still a strip club. When I'd last spoken to him he'd been training to become an Accountant. What had gone wrong? What had driven him to this? Was he really as happy as he'd told Mom in his notes?

# Chapter One

*The Past*

**LIAM**

It had been seven months since I'd left home and my gut still burnt and twisted every time I thought about the family I'd lost. No....not lost, I'd thrown them away with my stupid, vindictive behavior. I'd conspired with a man who ended a baby's life and almost the life of the woman my brother had fallen in love with. Not to mention, I'd almost cost my brother *his* life as well. What kind of person was I? How had I let jealousy eat away at me until I'd come to that point?

Foster, one of the boys who lived and hung out on the street, ambled up to me. "Hey, Liam. You working tonight?"

I stubbed my cigarette out under my heel. Yep, I took up smoking not long after I left home. "Nope, got the night off. What are you doing?"

"We're hitting Calibers."

"Who?"

"Simon, Gavin and me. Join us?"

"Dunno, I don't like Gavin. I don't trust him."

"Aaw, so he sells a few drugs. He's harmless."

"More than a few. It's not a scene I wanna get involved in. Besides, I'm not even eighteen and he's twenty-eight, older than my brother. Fuck, he's a grown man."

"What difference does that make?"

"A lot. He should be making an honest living, maybe married with kids. Instead, he's shagging anything on two legs and dealing drugs. I know I've fallen but I'm not gonna fall that far. I'm working hard to put together a good life. I'll give it a miss, but thanks." I started to walk away.

"Your loss. I hear a few girls from Bellini's will be there."

I spun back to face Foster. "Bellini's girls? You know those fucking chicks will spread their legs for anyone and it's common knowledge they're not clean. Be careful."

"Yeah, whatever. You're worse than my mother and fuck, I left home to get away from her and her fucking nagging."

"Foster, you're fourteen years old, stay away from them *and* Gavin. You'll find yourself in more trouble than you can handle if you don't."

He flicked me the bird and swaggered off in the opposite direction. I strode to the front door of my apartment block. It was always open and half the time, hung from the hinges. The hall was filthy and reeked of alcohol, vomit, urine and shit. I had to deal with it; this place was all I could afford and after what I'd done, it's what I deserved.

My apartment was on the third floor. The elevator was fucked and had been for eight years, so I'd been told. When I arrived home from the restaurant after working the late shift, it wasn't unusual to find several bodies sprawled out drunk or drugged on the steps. It was early afternoon though and the stairs were clear for a change. I took them two at a time and reached the third floor with no effort at all. I guess six months of traipsing up and down had improved my fitness.

I unlocked my apartment, stepped inside and locked the door behind me. In this neighborhood you never knew what to expect. I threw my cigarettes, lighter and key on the kitchen bench and headed for the bedroom. My only furniture was an old wooden, second-hand bed and a small flat screen television. They were both in the bedroom.

After stripping off, I flopped onto the bed naked and flipped on the television. Somehow, I'd managed to get into cable and had taken to watching the porn channel. An afternoon jack-off was nothing unusual as I watched some chick on the screen being fucked or two men going at it. Men turned me on almost as much as women. Who was I kidding? Men turned me on a hell of a lot more than women.

A moan filled the room as the screen came to life. A blonde was being ass fucked and the dude was fucking huge. My cock stood to attention and I fondled the length. Jewels of pre-cum erupted from my slit and I used them as lube. While one hand toyed with my hardening dick, the other tortured my nipples. I liked a bit of pain, it turned me on and reminded me I was still alive.

The couple on screen were fucking hard and fast; the bedhead banged the wall. My cock pulsated in my hand but I needed more. I reached out, grabbed my vibe and after lubing it up, slid it into my ass. As soon as I flicked the switch, my entire body came to life. My cock danced around so much; my fucking hand had to chase it from one side of my belly to the other. More pre-cum appeared and my hand spread the thick, sticky liquid over my length.

The couple on screen was really going at it and I noticed he'd pushed a vibe into his own ass. My stomach contracted. My dick was so hard it would have rivaled petrified wood. The vibe was pressing against my prostate and it was all too much. I exploded. Pulsating jets of cum decorated my belly and chest. I quivered and shook. Every fucking orgasm was better than the one before. I glanced at the television in time to watch the two fuck buddies shatter and my dick hardened again. The next orgasm blew me away. Tears filled my eyes with the stimulation and jet after jet of warm cum shot onto my belly. When I was finally spent, I withdrew the vibe and fell into a deep sleep.

***

"For fuck sake, wait!" I yelled out while hopping around and trying to get a leg into my sweats. I was gonna pound whoever was at the door if they banged on it one more time. I glanced at my watch and saw it was six in the evening. I'd been asleep for almost four hours.

With sweats firmly in place, I hurried to the door and reached for the knob. The fucking thing didn't move and I remembered it was locked. You'd think I'd know to grab the key first after being here for so long. I unlocked the door and flung it back with enough force that it hit the wall, bounced off and almost hit me on the rebound. The abuse I was ready to sling died in my throat. I felt my mouth drop open. Why the fuck was my brother at my door and how the fuck had he found me?

"Liam, close your mouth and invite me in." Steve strode in and I closed the door as he stood in the center of my living room, taking in the bareness of the apartment. "I love what you've done with the place, you must give me the number of your decorator."

I finally found my voice. "Always the smart ass. What the fuck do you want?"

"I want to talk, like we should have months ago."

"Got nothing to talk about."

"Very well. Sit your ass on the floor." Steve glanced around the small space. "It appears there's nowhere else to sit. I'll talk. *You'll listen.*"

"You're wasting your time. I wanna be left alone."

"Yeah, we kinda figured that out when we didn't hear a word from you. It's breaking Mom's heart. Hear me out and if you still want to be left alone, I'll honor your wishes." Steve plonked himself on the filthy, partially rotten boards, which did a piss poor job of imitating a floor.

I sighed and gave in. One thing I knew about my brother - when he set his mind to something, there was no changing it. I sat down opposite and crossed my long legs. "Do you want a water or a beer?"

"Drinking, Liam? How do you manage to get alcohol, you're underage? On second thoughts, don't answer that, I don't want to know. No, nothing for me, thank you."

"What do you want to say?"

"Mom and Dad were devastated when they read your note after you left. They've been searching for you for months. Dad hired a private investigator and we got the news the day before yesterday that he'd found you."

"Humph, I notice they didn't come."

"They asked me to. They seemed to think if you see I've forgiven you for what happened, you'll forgive them and come home."

"Not happening. Fuck, you could have been fucking killed and Keegan lost her fucking baby and almost her own life because of me. *You* might forgive me but I'll never forgive myself."

Steve reached out and placed his hand on my arm. I flinched and moved away.

"It's in the past, Liam. Keegan and I are getting married and we need to move on. I knew you were feeling jealous – for want of a better word - of me. I knew you were angry and felt like Mom and Dad favored me. I didn't take the opportunity to speak to any of you about it. I dismissed it as normal childhood behavior. When I look back, I can see Mom and Dad treated me like

I was special and I'm so sorry I didn't realize it at the time and say something. Now I'm out of home, things will be different. I've discussed with Mom and Dad how you must have been feeling and they realize now, they didn't give you the time and attention you needed...that you had every right to expect."

"It was always about you, Steve. How you'd risen from the gutter and could achieve anything you put your mind to. Mom always saying how much she loved you because you chose *her* to be your mother. You were her special son. Dad saying he was so proud of you. How you were never any trouble, unlike me. I wanted their love. I wanted to be special too. No matter what I did, I wasn't good enough. I wasn't you." Tears dripped from my eyes and when I glanced at my brother, he was crying too.

"I'm so very sorry. I didn't know you felt so bad. I didn't know how much you were hurting."

"I *was* hurting, Steve and I wanted you to hurt too. I'm sorry for how it all turned out."

"Will you forgive us? Will you come back with me, let us make it up to you?"

I swallowed hard. More than anything, I wanted to go home, but I couldn't. Not yet. Maybe not ever. "No, I won't come home. I have a job here waiting tables. Mrs. Chin, who owns the restaurant, is a Certified Accountant and she's helping me to get my degree. She said I'm very clever with numbers and would make an excellent Accountant. She's the first person who has told me I'm smart. I love the numbers, the theory and practice behind accountancy. She's paying for me to go to college four hours a day, four days a week and I work in the restaurant at night. She pays me enough to cover my rent and a few items, the rest goes toward college and books."

"I don't know what to say. Mom and Dad would pay for you to go to college in Paxton. They would be so proud of you."

"It's too late, Steve. They weren't there when I needed them the most. I won't turn my back on Mrs. Chin, she's done so much for me."

Steve nodded. I thought..... *hoped*, he might understand.

"Word on the street is, you ride a bike?"

"I do. Mrs. Chin's only son died a few years back from some disease. She knew I walked from here to the restaurant, which is five miles away and offered me his bike which had been sitting in their garage. Something else I owe her for. Tell Mom and Dad, I do love them and maybe one day, I'll visit. For now, I want and *need* to be left alone."

"Can we send you money, buy you furniture?" Steve waved his arm around my empty apartment.

"No, Steve. Please, leave me alone."

Steve stood and offered his hand which I accepted. He pulled me to my feet and into a bear hug. When I pulled away, I noted the fresh tears in his eyes.

"Can I visit now and again or call you?"

I shake my head, no.

"Will you call Mom and Dad to let them know you're okay? Once a week, please? Mom is devastated."

I sighed and dragged fingers through my hair. "Once a month I'll send a note, that's it."

"Thank you."

Steve hugged me again and I showed him out. After he'd gone, I locked the door, slid down the wall to the floor, buried my head in my hands and sobbed my heart out. I knew I'd done the right thing but it still hurt like hell. One day, I *would* go back and see my family, but when *I* was ready, not when they were.

# Chapter Two

After Steve left and I'd cried myself dry, I headed for the shower. I still had dried cum on my belly and I was embarrassed to think my brother might have noticed it. When I reached the bathroom, I glanced in the mirror as I slid the sweats down my legs. I looked like something the cat had dragged in and felt like it too. I'd spent months pushing what I'd done into the dark recesses of my mind and now, seeing Steve, had brought every minute detail to the forefront.

I flipped the faucet on and stepped under the piss poor excuse for a shower. The water was barely above a trickle and only just off cold. As I washed, I wondered about what I should do. I knew if I stayed here it would only be a matter of time before Mom and Dad turned up on my doorstep and demanded I return home. It was disappointing, I was finally headed in the right direction. Why couldn't they have just let me go, forgotten about me?

I turned off the faucet and stepped out, grabbed a towel and dried myself off. I didn't bother with the sweats on the floor. Instead, I padded through to the bedroom and grabbed a clean pair from an old set of drawers which was barely holding together. I didn't bother with underwear. A t-shirt was next, followed by a pair of running shoes. I was all set to head out to find something to eat. Nope, I didn't cook – couldn't, actually. I'd usually pick up something from one of the dozens of takeaway shops or, on the nights I worked, I'd bring home some of the leftovers. Most of the time I ate healthy, but now and again, I indulged in junk food.

I grabbed my keys and wallet from the table, before heading out onto the street. Tonight, it would be *Allamars* for Turkish. Something spicy, maybe.

***

It wasn't quite seven in the evening and drunken bodies were already scattered on the steps of the apartment building in various states of unconsciousness. I had no idea who any of them were. I generally kept to myself. The only reason I knew Foster was because I'd found him badly beaten up one night. It was also the same night I'd met Simon and Gavin. Simon was hovering over the kid as he lay in the gutter unconscious and Gavin was picking Foster's pockets – he quickly found out there was nothing to be picked. I'd managed to talk them out of doing anything they'd regret and had carried Foster back upstairs to my apartment where I'd taken care of him for the next few days. Unfortunately, I hadn't been able to talk him into going home or staying with me and he'd headed back onto the streets. Somehow, he'd fallen in with Simon and Gavin and I worried about what they'd get him involved in. Ha! Me, a *murderer,* worrying about what someone else might be pulled into. Maybe caring about someone else was my way of seeking redemption.

I picked my way over the bodies to find more sprawled in the lobby. I thanked God every night that Mrs. Chin had taken me under her wing, I had no doubt I would have been one of those bodies if it hadn't been for her guidance. She was a tiny slip of a woman, originally from Taiwan. I'd been living in an alcove at the back of the restaurant for four days when she'd found me. I'd chosen the space because it was well hidden from the street and I'd quickly found out, to my relief, that nobody bothered with it. Mrs. Chin had been putting the trash out when she'd noticed me and approached. I was cold, tired, hungry and soaked through from recent rain. I'd almost admitted to myself, I was scared and was on the verge of heading home to beg for my parent's forgiveness. *Almost.*

Mrs. Chin had 'ordered' me to my feet and marched me inside. I'd dropped my wet duffel bag on the floor in the kitchen, not wanting it to drip all over the place. The tiny woman had immediately snatched it up and ordered me to follow her. I quickly discovered, she liked to give orders. She threw my duffel onto the floor of what looked like a laundry room and led me upstairs.

"This is where we live. I'll show you to the shower. You're about the same size as my husband – Jiāháo so, I'll get you some clean, dry clothes."

The woman spoke remarkably good English and I later found out, she'd come here as a child and had been educated in our system. Her husband, a kindly man much older than her, had come as an adult and spoke very few words in our language.

I'd showered and been ordered to take a seat at their small wooden table. I'd eaten more food that night than I'd thought myself capable of. The soft bed in the guest room had allowed me to get the best night's sleep I'd had in days.

Over the next few days, I'd helped in the restaurant by waiting tables. I'd found I really enjoyed it and when Mrs. Chin offered me a job which included medical, I jumped at the offer. When we weren't working, Mrs. Chin and I spent hours talking. I discovered I could tell her anything and before long, I'd told her about what had happened. She tried to get me to go home, or at the very least, to contact my parents, but I refused. I didn't deserve to live in their beautiful home with the beach at their back door. To have all the niceties of life handed to me. I deserved to suffer and battle to make a new life for myself. I needed to prove to myself, I wasn't as evil as I believed.

On the days I wasn't working but Mrs. Chin was, I combed the area for an apartment I could afford. There wasn't much on offer and I eventually signed on the best of a really bad lot. Mrs. Chin had disapproved when I'd told her I was moving out ten days after she'd ordered me into her home. I'd explained, I needed to be on my own and if it broke me, it was only what I deserved. Reluctantly, she'd let me go after making me promise I'd return if things got too hard. I'd made the promise but it was one I'd had no intention of keeping.

A few weeks later, I'd made us both a coffee – the limit of my culinary abilities - and sat down to join her at a small table in a corner of the large commercial kitchen. She was busy with the accounts and frustrated that she'd become stuck. Leaning over her shoulder, I peered at the figures and quickly pointed out where the problem was. After that, Mrs. Chin had insisted I come into work an hour early every day and work on the books with her. Two months ago, she'd secretly enrolled me in community college in an Accountancy course. I had argued, begged and pleaded for her to allow me to pay her back from my pay each week but she'd staunchly refused. In the end, I'd accepted her generous offer and decided the best way to repay her kindness was to get the best grades possible. So far, I'd proven myself to be a consistent honors student and I knew she took great pride in bragging about it to her friends.

***

I pushed through the door to the outside and into the warm evening air. It was permeated with a mixture of cooking smells from local restaurants and street vendors and washed over me. The warm weather always brought people out and the walkways were busy. *Allamars* was less than a block from my apartment and I managed to thread my way through the crowds to reach the place in a few minutes. My mouth watered when I stepped inside to be bombarded by the scents of a myriad of Turkish spices. I waited patiently in line until it was my turn to step up to the ordering counter.

"Liam, how are you?" the owner, Mr. Adivar asked.

"I'm good, Mr. Adivar. You?"

He sighed and frowned at me slightly. Every time I came in he asked that I call him, Nadip and every time, I explained I was raised to treat my elders with respect which meant I referred to him by his formal name. Tonight, he didn't bother to chastise me.

"I'm very well. Bahri was accepted into college to study Medicine."

Bahri was his beloved grandson, the son of his only daughter. It was obvious the man was extremely proud.

"Congratulations. From what you have told me, he'll make a fine doctor."

"And, you? How is college for you?"

"I'm doing well. It helps that I love the course, too."

Mr. Adivar nodded and as there were other people waiting, I moved away from our small talk.

"I'll have the Iskender Chicken, with yoghurt and pita bread, please."

My order was ready in a matter of moments and after farewelling the gentleman, I headed back onto the street. The bag with my order swung slightly in my left hand.

By the time I was securely locked in my apartment again, my stomach was grumbling. I headed through to the bedroom, placed the bag on my bed, switched on the television and settled back to enjoy my food.

\*\*\*

For the next few days, I spent the nights tossing and turning and the days, being unable to concentrate. Mrs. Chin suspected something was wrong but she didn't push to know what was troubling me, for which I was grateful. Fear, that Steve would return, consumed me. He'd said he forgave me and maybe he did, but I knew Keegan never would. Eventually, I'd decided I should bring an end to my pathetic excuse for a life. So, shortly after his visit, I'd sliced my wrists. I'd fallen asleep and woken to find the blood had stopped flowing and I was still very much alive – I hadn't cut deep enough. Since then, the war had raged in my head. The only thing which stopped me from attempting it again was the fear of never seeing my parents again. I didn't want them yet, but I knew the day would come when I did. To say I was fucked in the head was an understatement.

A week after Steve's visit, I'd made the decision to pack up what little I had and leave. I'd felt guilty about not telling Mrs. Chin but I couldn't stand the thought of watching her heart break. Even though I didn't deserve to have her care about me, I knew she did.

I headed straight for the bus station in Linton and hopped the first bus which pulled in. I'd decided, wherever it terminated was where I would set up home. At least I had a few dollars saved and hopefully I could afford a better place than the last one.

The bus was headed to Nollet, about twenty-five miles from Linton. It was the major city in our area and we'd always referred to it as 'downtown.' I dozed on and off, getting some much-needed sleep as the bus wound its way through the streets to the terminus in Nollet.

Night had begun falling when I stepped onto the pavement in a seedier part of the city. I was hungry and exhausted so, my priorities were a takeaway place and cheap motel. I found both a few feet away in the 'clubs' district.

After I grabbed a burger and bottle of water, I headed to the motel the street vendor had pointed out and checked in for a week. The owner gave me a special discount rate for staying seven nights. The place turned out to be cheaper than I'd thought and when I'd pushed open the door to my room, I was surprised with how clean it was. It was just the one room with another door on the opposite wall which was open. I could see it led through to a bathroom. It would certainly do until I found somewhere more permanent.

I dropped my duffel on the floor, flopped onto the bed, turned on the television and proceeded to get stuck into the burger. It wasn't half bad. There was cable at the motel so I immediately switched onto the porn channel before heading to take a shower. When I returned, clean and dried, it was in time to find two rather cute guys going at it. My cock thickened and stood up against my belly. Pre-cum was already dripping and I spread it over the length before standing and grabbing the vibrator and lube from my bag. I threw back the covers, stretched out on the sheet and fisted my excited cock.

I stroked languidly as I watched one man sink balls deep into the other while pulling his head back by the hair. They were both moaning and groaning their pleasure and I found myself moaning softly with them as shivers raced down my spine and tingles zapped into every extremity – signs I was ready to explode. And, explode I did.

String after string of thick, creamy cum decorated my belly while the orgasm seemed to hold me in its grip for what seemed like an eternity. When I finally descended, I turned back to the television to see the men had switched places, the other man now had his cock shoved up the ass of the first. When my cock hardened again I groaned, I was too fucking exhausted for more.

I switched off the television, plunging the room into darkness and for the first time in a week, with no threat of my family finding me hanging over my head, I drifted into a deep, dreamless sleep.

# Chapter Three

I was woken around eight the following morning by a loud argument outside my door. I guessed it was to be expected in this part of town. They were probably drunks leaving one of the nightclubs. When the argument became heated, I couldn't resist a peek through the window and was alarmed to see a large, well-built man holding a smaller man by the scruff of the neck. They were standing outside a club called – *The Velvet Post*. I knew I shouldn't interfere but my commonsense fled and I found myself pulling on sweats and heading for the door.

"Hey! What's going on?" I shouted as I checked the street and hurried across to where the men were still arguing.

They both spun toward me and I watched as two sets of eyes checked out my naked chest. The larger man released his hold on the smaller man and the freed man brushed at his crumpled jacket before he turned and smiled my way.

"Well, hello gorgeous. What's your name?" The smaller man stepped toward me and even separated by a few feet, I could smell the stench of alcohol on his breath.

The larger man pushed the small one and he stumbled a few steps down the pavement. "Get out of here, Rick, your wife will be wondering where the hell you are."

The small man grumbled about catching up with me later and I watched as he weaved his way down the road.

"Will he get home okay?" I had no idea why I should care.

"Yeah, sorry about that. At least once a week he gets fired up when I tell him it's time to leave." He held out his hand and I noticed how long and slender his fingers were. "I'm Jake Brown, co-owner of the Velvet Post. You're new around here."

It was a statement rather than a question. The man was fucking gorgeous -a little taller than my own six feet two inches, close cropped blonde hair with golden brown highlights and smoky gray eyes. His skin was unmarked and had a slight golden tinge to it. I was really glad at that moment that I was wearing sweats because my cock swelled to epic proportions. Well, not quite, but it was certainly interested. I'd never had such a strong reaction when meeting a man. Or, when meeting a woman for that matter.

"Um, sorry. Liam Masters. Yeah, came in on the bus last night."

Jake looked me up and down again and my cock chose the exact moment his eyes were at my groin to flinch. I knew he hadn't missed the movement when his previously light gray eyes darkened to the color of storm clouds. I felt my cheeks heat with embarrassment and instinctively dropped my hands to my groin. He licked his lips before he lifted his eyes back to mine.

"Don't hide what you have, Babe. From where I'm standing, it looks rather impressive. Do you dance?"

"Dance?"

"Yeah - pole dance."

I relaxed enough to laugh. "In your dreams, I've got two left feet when it comes to dance and if I attempted to dance on a pole, I'd break my fucking neck."

"Have you ever tried it? With your body, you could make good money."

"No, I've never even thought about it. My previous job was as a waiter and I was studying accounting."

Jake's eyebrows flew up to meet his hairline. I didn't know whether it was because I'd said I was a waiter or studying accounting.

"Will you come inside and have a coffee with me. I'd like to chat further and out here in the street isn't exactly appropriate when I'd like to offer you a job." Jake stretched out his arm, indicating the entry door to the club.

*A job? Work with this beautiful man? Could do worse.* Maybe I could wait tables in the club, they did have tables after all. I could learn to serve drinks. It couldn't be that much different to serving food.

"Yeah, why not?"

\*\*\*

J ake led me inside and locked the heavy metal door behind him. I felt a shiver slide down my spine and the hairs stood up on the back of my neck when I realized, I was locked inside with a man who had at least a couple of inches and at least thirty pounds on me. The fear, as I recognized it, only lasted a moment. Inside the club, there were three other men who were clearing away glasses and cleaning tables. Dressed in pants which looked like they'd been painted on, they left very little to the imagination. I felt my eyes widen. What kind of club was this?

I need to explain. I hadn't lived on the streets long enough to 'get educated' or obtain 'street smarts.' In many ways, I was rather naïve – sex was one of them. I'd fucked a couple of women but had never openly ogled other men. I'd also never found the courage to have sex with a man, even though they were definitely my preference.

Jake must have noticed my obvious confusion. When it hit me that this was a gay club and my eyes widened, he laughed. A deep, booming laugh which I instantly thought I wanted to hear more of. My face heated to the point that beads of sweat formed over my top lip.

Jake held two fingers up and a man clearing tables nearby nodded before moving away. "Come through to my office and I'll explain."

I followed him through the club and past a raised stage where two men I hadn't previously noticed were performing some amazing moves around a couple of poles. I hadn't realized I'd stopped to watch, mesmerized by the beautiful men, until Jake placed his hand on the top of my arm.

"That's Chris and Pedro. Beautiful, aren't they?"

I nodded. "Yes, they are."

"Coffees up." The man who'd been clearing tables spoke as he brushed past us. He held a tray in his hands.

Jake urged me forward and I dragged my gaze from the men on stage to follow the man with the coffee. I needed one. I was definitely suffering with testosterone overload thanks to the bevy of beautiful men so close at hand.

The coffees were placed on the desk in an office we'd entered and the man turned toward me, his hand outstretched. I slid my palm into his and we shook.

"Hi, I'm Joey. Welcome to the best club on the east side." He raked his eyes over my body and raised an eyebrow. "Very nice." He ran his fingertips over my upper chest and I shivered as tingles streaked down my spine. "Very, very nice. Do you always make a habit of walking around bare-chested?"

"Liam and no, I don't. I heard arguing outside my motel room and rushed out with only my sweats on."

Joey addressed Jake. "Rick?"

Jake nodded.

"Guess he argued with the little woman last night." Joey turned back to me. "Every time Rick argues with his wife, he comes in here, gets plastered and then argues with whomever tells him to go home."

I nodded in understanding.

"Anything else, Boss?" Joey asked.

"No, thanks, Joey."

"I'll catch you later. Oh, and Honey, if you don't want to be snapped up by the wrong man, I suggest you dress before going outside in future," he said to me before he nodded at Jake, left the office and closed the door with a soft click.

***

"Have a seat and we'll talk."

Jake sat behind his desk and I dropped into a chair opposite. He pushed one of the mugs toward me along with sugar sachets and cream. I tipped a portion of cream into my mug, stirred and took a sip. I couldn't contain the moan which escaped my lips. I really loved my first cup of the day.

Jake laughed before sipping his own – black, no sugar I noted.

"He's right you know, you need to be careful around this district. A lot of men are on the hunt for a quick fuck and with your body, you'll be a prime target.

"What makes you think I'm gay?"

"Babe, I've never had a straight man get a boner like you did when we were outside talking."

As I sipped at the coffee, I felt heat burn my cheeks. I pretty much knew he'd noticed my reaction but it didn't lessen the embarrassment.

"Do you always blush bright red when you're caught out?"

"It's not often I get caught out."

"Experienced?"

"At what?"

He pierced me with his gray eyes.

"You know what."

I lowered my head and again, heat crept over my cheeks.

"Ah, I think I've found myself a virgin. A rarity in this part of town. How old are you?"

"I'll be eighteen in just under five months' time and I'm not a virgin. I've fucked women before."

Jake cocked his head to the side and studied me.

"Hmm, not men though. Closet?"

I dropped my eyes to the coffee and stared at it like it was fascinating.

"Lee."

My head snapped up, I'd only ever been called Lee by Mom. Jake relaxed back in his chair and folded his arms across his broad chest.

"This won't work if you're not honest with me. I'd like to offer you a job but first off, I'll ask you a bunch of questions and then you can ask me anything you want to know about me. We're like a family to each other here. We don't drink to excess. We don't do drugs, but if you do, I can guarantee you'll be found out and fired. We don't lie to each other. We look out for each other and if one of us is in trouble, we take care of them. Agreed?"

"Agreed." This was like no job interview I'd ever had before, not that I'd had many.

"Okay. Virgin, and you know I'm talking about men, don't you?"

"Yes," I whispered.

"Closet?"

"I guess so. I haven't hidden the fact I like guys but I haven't exactly admitted I'm gay either."

"You've been confused and afraid, that's the reason you tried fucking women. Does your family know?"

"No, we're....um, we don't talk. I've done some things in the past I'm ashamed of."

"Illegal?"

"No."

"Then we'll get past it. Drugs?"

"Never. I used to smoke but gave up recently."

"Drink?"

"No."

"You obviously work out."

"I eat healthy most of the time and I do squats, sit-ups, lift weights when I have the opportunity to sneak into a gym."

"Sneak?"

"I haven't been able to afford to join one."

"Not a problem, we have our own downstairs. The men here use it to keep themselves fit."

"I guess you don't have a girlfriend or boyfriend."

"No."

"Why did you come here?"

"My brother found out where I was living and wanted me to go back home. I wasn't ready and I didn't want my family turning up on the doorstep again."

"So, you ran?"

"Yeah."

"I'll ask again. Did you do something illegal?"

I lifted my head and locked eyes with Jake. "No, but it should have been."

Jake nodded. "Your turn."

"How old are you?"

"Twenty-Six."

"You said you co-owned the club?"

"Yep, my brother Roan owns it with me, he's seven years older than me. We bought it five years ago."

"Do your dancers get fucked by clients?"

"Whoa, you get right to the point, don't you? No, they don't. They give private lap dances to clients they have a special bond with but it's always their choice."

"Do you have a ....friend?"

"No, I'm not in a relationship and before you ask, everyone here is gay."

"What do you want from me?"

"I want you to dance."

I laughed. "I already told you, I can't."

"Pedro and Chris can teach you."

"Why?"

"Why, what?"

"Why do you want me to dance?"

"Because I think you're stunning and you'll attract more clients to our club."

"It looked like it's already successful."

"It is. Very, but if we don't continue to try new people, new things, we won't continue to grow."

"What if I'm no good?"

"Then, I'll shove you away in my office to do the fucking books. I hate them and so does Roan. You can't wait tables, we're licensed and you're underage. On stage you'll look a hell of a lot older than you are with the lights on you. You're well developed for a kid of eighteen."

I finished my coffee and pushed the mug away from me.

"Almost eighteen. Okay, I'll give it a try on two conditions."

"They are?"

"I won't ever fuck clients. I won't give lap dances and if I fail, you employ me as your book-keeper."

"That's three but done."

Jake offered his hand and we shook.

"I'll get the paperwork drawn up. You're not technically old enough to be working here. Our local police like you to be at least eighteen but I'll take a chance. If we get caught, I'll pay the fine and shove you in the office until after your birthday. I can't register you for medical cover until after your birthday either but if anything happens, or you get sick, I'll pay for whatever you need."

"That'll be in the paperwork?"

"You're not very trusting, are you?"

"Haven't had a reason to be. What's the pay?"

"Eight hundred a week plus whatever you make in tips."

I felt my eyes widen. Eight. Fucking. Hundred. Dollars! I'd earned three hundred with Mrs. Chin and I thought that was pretty good. "What do the others make in tips?"

"Without the lap dances, around two thousand a week."

"Fuck!"

"I expect you'll make a lot more. Pedro is a brilliant choreographer and I have something special in mind for you."

Fuck! Right at that moment, I was begging every power I knew to help me become a passable dancer.

"You don't have anywhere to live?"

"No, like I said, I only arrived last night."

"You don't know the area, I'll help you."

I don't know why I wanted his help but I found myself agreeing to it.

"I have seven days in the motel so how about we check out the estate agents on Monday?"

"Sounds good. I have Sunday and Monday off this week but I'm covering for Roan for a couple of hours this Monday as he has a meeting at three o'clock. We'll have plenty of time to check out apartments and have lunch before I have to get to the club."

"Okay. When do you want me to start?"

"Now."

"N..n..now?"

"Now."

Jake stood, crossed to the door and called out for Joey.

"Joey, bring me a string."

Within seconds, I watched as Joey handed a flimsy scrap of black material to Jake and he again closed the door.

"Put these on and I'll introduce you to Chris and Pedro."

I accepted the black G-string and laughed. "There's no way this will cover me."

"It stretches and will cover what needs to be covered. Put it on."

I hesitated, unsure of what I should do. I mean, wasn't he going to turn around to give me some privacy?

"I'm not turning around. You'll be changing with the rest of the men in the change room so you may as well get used to stripping off with others around. It's only me so, it's a good starting point. Put them on."

I'd never thought I was self-conscious about my body but sliding my shoes off and then my sweats in front of the gorgeous man before me, embarrassed the fucking hell out of me. Fortunately, my insecurity meant my cock remained soft and didn't embarrass me further by getting hard. I hurriedly pulled on the G-string, Jake was right, it did cover me. Just.

I stood waiting for him to tell me what to do next and when I gazed into his eyes, I could see the want, the lust which filled his smoky gray depths. My cock did betray me at that moment and Jake's eyes flicked to my hardening appendage. Once again, heat crawled into my cheeks. If I was to make any kind of future for myself here, I was going to have to temper my emotions.

# Chapter Four

**JAKE**

When I'd first spotted Liam from the corner of my eye as he crossed the street to where I was arguing with Rick, I'd thought I'd died and gone to heaven. The ripple of his bared chest muscles as he walked had caused my cock to come alive for the first time in what seemed like forever.

His hair stuck out at all angles and it was obvious he'd only just climbed out of bed. As my eyes trailed down his body, I caught the flinch of his dick and I instantly wanted him. Then, he'd blushed and I'd wanted him even more. I'd had to take stock of myself at that point. Although very much a man, it was obvious he was far too young for me.

His voice was husky and deep, setting fireworks off in every cell of my body. I couldn't figure the effect this young man was having on me. I wanted to spend more time with him to work it out. I had never liked puzzles or being confused and this man was turning me inside out. I wanted to know why.

I didn't usually employ guys under the age of twenty-one, mainly because after being on stage, they could mingle with the clientele and hopefully draw more money from them for both the club and themselves. The *Velvet Post* was a successful venture and netted my brother and I a tidy sum, most of which we invested in real estate or blue-ribbon stock. It had made us very wealthy men and we had enough money to last for a few lifetimes. We didn't have a manager. Instead, we worked four days on, three days off. When one of us took a break for a couple of weeks, one of the men we employed would step up to help us out. Usually Joey. It worked incredibly well. Every man working the club had been with us since the opening and we all looked out for each other.

I'd invited Lee into the club on the pretense of employing him when all I'd wanted was to spend more time getting to know the young man. He was tall, only a couple of inches shorter than my own six feet five inches and had the body of an elite athlete – every muscle perfectly defined. His vivid green eyes were electrifying, but there was a deep sadness in them which had me wondering what secrets they hid. That he had been touched by tragedy, I didn't doubt for one moment.

When we'd entered the club, I'd seen his eyes widen at the sight of our men clearing tables in their body hugging pants. They were comfortable with their bodies, as they should be. They all had bodies our clients drooled over nightly. Chris and Pedro had been up on stage practicing a routine they'd put together a couple of weeks ago and I'd waited while Lee watched with interest. Although I'd first intended to ask him to take over the books, a job Roan and I detested, I really wanted him up on stage where his body deserved to be seen.

I decided I would gently coax him into at least trying to perform, but I had no intention of forcing him. If it wasn't what he wanted, I would return to my original idea of having him do the books. I couldn't understand why I wanted to keep him around. Why did he set my body on fire? I'd only just met him. Yes, he had a body to die for but I'd seen other men who were almost as perfect. Hell, I had them working here and had been around them all regularly since we'd opened the club. Not one of them appealed to me in *that* way. Not one of them made me feel like I wanted to drag them into the nearest bed and fuck them until they couldn't stand up. No, there was something intriguing about Lee and I aimed to find out what it was.

When I'd told Lee to put on the G-string, he'd looked at me in horror and insisted there wasn't enough of it to contain him. I'd scoffed at the statement, insisting it would stretch, but when he stripped off and stood naked, I almost swallowed my tongue. Even I had my doubts it would fit at that point.

His dick had hardened slightly under my perusal and fuck me if Lee hadn't blushed again. He hadn't lied, this man was certainly a virgin and not accustomed to being on display. Would I be the one to educate him? I chastized myself for being so ridiculous and reminded myself again, he was far too young for me. And, he was to be my employee.

***

I opened the door of the office and extended my hand for Lee to head out first. For the second time in mere moments, I almost swallowed my tongue when I caught sight of his firm, round ass. My cock thickened painfully. This man was gonna be the death of me.

He headed toward the stage but cast a glance over his shoulder just as I licked the drool from my lips. Fuck.

"See something you like?"

Shit, for someone so young and inexperienced, he was certainly direct. I was saved from embarrassment when Pedro jumped from the stage and sashayed toward us.

"Boss, new dancer?"

Chris joined him seconds later. They were certainly glued at the hip these days, I wondered if they were more than just friends. It didn't matter, their relationship was none of my business as long as it didn't cause problems at the club.

"Pedro, Chris – this is Liam….."

"I like Lee," he interrupted.

"Lee it is then. He's never danced before but I'm hoping with some instruction from you two, he'll be able to manage the Devil and Angel routine. The ones you two showed me a few moves from but didn't want to do."

Lee snapped his eyes my way, a questioning frown on his face but Pedro had noticed and answered his unasked question before I could open my mouth.

"We dance together, Lee, the Devil and Angel routines are solo. Center stage, total focus. Not for us."

"Why the fuck would you think I can dance up there on my own?"

Lee had jammed his hands on his narrow hips and stood glaring at me.

"I have a gut feeling you have more talent than you know and my gut is never wrong."

"It's wrong this time. I can't get up there and dance alone. Fuck, I don't know if I could dance in front of a crowd along with half a dozen guys."

He turned to walk away and I grabbed him by the arm.

"Please, will you at least give it a try for a few days. I give you my word, I'll employ you in the office if it doesn't work out."

Pedro, bless his heart took Lee's hand and started leading him away. Chris hung behind and I watched as he checked out Lee's ass. I wanted to thump him but instead, I got over myself and headed to the bar for a soda water. I rarely drank alcohol and it was far too early for the occasional one I did indulge in. After helping myself to a bottle from the fridge and twisting the cap off, I hoisted myself onto a stool to watch.

The three men bounced up the steps at the side of the raised stage and headed for a pole at the center, it was one that raised out of the floor. The up and down feature hadn't been utilized for performances yet. The men had been content to leave it fixed in place. I knew the Devil and Angel routines required the dancer to rise through the floor amid smoke. My cock danced at the thought of watching Lee rise before an appreciative crowd before performing a variety of gravity defying tricks.

Electrical impulses zapped through every muscle of my body at the thought of him becoming my star attraction, watching him on stage, night after night. An unexpected jolt of jealousy flashed through me at the thought of men wanting to lay their hands all over him as he danced and gyrated for them. What the fuck was happening to me?

***

"Place your hand on the pole here….and……here." Pedro lifted Lee's hands and placed them on the pole where he wanted them. One above his head, arm outstretched, the other at waist level.

Pedro had chosen to use the center pole and I had an excellent view of all three men. While he stood off to one side instructing, Chris hovered behind. My view of Lee wasn't being blocked.

"Now, lift yourself up onto the pole using the strength of your arms."

As Lee flexed his muscles and what gorgeous muscles they were, Chris wrapped his arms around Lee's waist and helped by lifting him high onto the pole.

"Wrap your left leg around it and hold yourself in place," Chris instructed before removing his hands.

I stifled a laugh when Lee dropped straight back to the floor.

"Okay, try again." Pedro positioned Lee's hands again.

Three more slides down the pole followed and when Chris and Pedro doubled over in laughter, I joined in from the bar. What followed had all of us stunned and a few seconds later, I was full of concern.

Lee started to leave the stage and I didn't miss the glazed look in his eyes. Pedro grabbed for him but Lee shook him off before spinning around.

"Leave me the fuck alone, I can't do it. It's like everything else I've tried, I'm a failure. If you want someone to star in your show, it should be Steve – he can do anything. He was always perfect, it was no wonder no-one noticed me. No-one noticed what I *could* do, what *I* needed."

When he raced to leave the stage, I jumped from the stool and dashed toward him. Pedro and Chris were still on stage, a confused expression on their faces. I shook my head, indicating to them I'd take care of things.

I caught up with Lee halfway to my office where I guessed he was headed to grab his sweats. I entered the room right behind him and locked the door behind us. Lee was standing with his head against the wall and he was sobbing.

I quietly moved up behind him, spun him around and wrapped him in my arms. Initially he attempted to push me away but when he realized I wasn't letting go, he relaxed and sobbed into my chest.

"I've never been any good, Jake. You don't want me here."

When Lee attempted to push out of my arms, I tightened my hold.

"I have no idea what's in your past and why you've been running, but it needs to stop, Lee. You have to deal with whatever is torturing you or it'll destroy you. Let us help."

"I can't do it, Jake. I should have killed myself instead of leaving Linton. I don't deserve to be alive and happy after what I've done."

Okay, this was some deep shit. What the fuck had he done to make himself think he'd be better off dead?

It was obvious he hadn't done anything illegal, I'd asked him and he'd assured me he hadn't. I believed him.

Even though I didn't know a damn thing about Lee, I instinctively knew he was telling me the truth. What I'd said was true, he needed to stop running but was I right, could we help him?

I hoped for his sake we could because I currently had a deeply troubled young man in my arms and I was scared to death about what he might do next.

# Chapter Five

**LIAM**

Being held in Jake's arms made me feel safe, less evil. I wanted to stay there for the rest of my days, but this man was my new boss, *if* he decided not to tell me to piss off after my outburst, which he probably would. I knew I'd behaved like a five-year-old throwing a tantrum. Maybe everything was getting on top of me and I'd finally snapped when Chris and Pedro had started laughing at my failure. When I stopped sobbing, I pushed back from Jake's hold and wiped my eyes with the back of my hand.

"I'm sorry, I'll get dressed and get out of your way." I turned away to pick up my sweats from the brown leather couch where I'd placed them.

Jake gripped the top of my arm, drew me to the couch and sat me down. He crouched before me and brushed the stray hairs from my face.

"Listen to me. Please?"

I nodded.

"Pedro and Chris were probably laughing because they've been where you're at. None of our men had ever danced before they came here. Roan had to teach each one of them and I lost count of how many times they slid off the pole before they finally got the hang of it. It takes persistence. You slide off, you get back up and do it again. And, again. And, again. Until you finally master it. Once you do, you'll wonder why you found it so fucking difficult."

"Roan dances?"

"Not any more. He used to dance at a club on the west side of town. Roan had long ago finished college but preferred to dance instead of practicing as a Psychologist. Dance was his first love. When it was sold, the once decent club became a seedy hovel. The new owner plied his dancers with drugs so they'd allow the clients to fuck them. The dancers never got paid for those fucks and the owner made plenty. Roan loved to dance and the club scene in general, but he refused to get involved with that side of it. Needless to say, he was fired. When he talked to me about what had happened and said his dream was to one day have his own club, I suggested we purchase a building and set up our own establishment. One we could set up from scratch with dancers Roan could train. We both had a sizeable inheritance from our Grandmother, more than enough to start up a business. One where our men were only expected to dance. The rest was up to them but fucking between our dancers and clients on the premises was forbidden. If they did, the dancer would be sent on their way."

"What about you, what were you doing at the time?"

"I was almost finished college - Roan and I are both qualified Psychologists. While I completed my degree, Roan bought this building and started setting it up. I helped out when I was free."

Psychologist? I understood now why he was so insistent on helping me. Was I prepared to let a shrink get inside my head? My thoughts? A shrink who I had an attraction to? A shrink who seemed intent on being my boss? I'd have to think long and hard over it.

My fidgeting hands rested in my lap and when Jake gathered them in his and his knuckles brushed over my cock, it jumped in response. I felt my face heat when our eyes locked.

"Fuck, you're gorgeous when you blush."

I lowered my eyes but Jake placed a finger under my chin and lifted my face until I looked at him again.

"Lee, I give you my word, I'll never force you to do anything you don't want to, but I want you to give it another try. I also want you to promise me something."

"What?"

"I want your word that you won't try to kill yourself or run again. Let me help you deal with the guilt and whatever happened in your past. If you're not comfortable with me, talk to Roan or another professional. Please?"

I nodded but saw in Jake's eyes, he wanted me to voice my promise out loud.

"I'll talk to you but I need time."

"Okay, I'm here when you're ready. Now, will we go back out and try again?"

"Yes," I whispered. For some reason, I wanted to please this man.

I knew next to nothing about Jake so, what was the strange hold he seemed to have over me?

\*\*\*

I noticed the men who'd been cleaning the tables had left when I went back out into the club. I climbed the stairs back onto the stage where Pedro and Chris had returned to their own practice. When I approached, they immediately headed toward me, concerned expressions on their faces.

"Everything okay?" Pedro asked.

"Yeah. I'm sorry for the meltdown."

Chris patted me on the back. "You should have seen Dixon when he first started. Man, we thought he'd tear the pole out of the ground he'd get so angry."

Pedro laughed. "Remember when he ripped his G-string off and stormed through the club to the dressing room butt naked?"

Chris nodded. "Yeah, when he reached the dressing room, he pulled on another G-string, stormed back up here and performed like he was a professional."

"We remind him about it from time to time when his head gets a bit overblown about a good performance. Don't tell him I said so, but he's fucking beautiful on stage," Pedro admitted.

Jake placed his hand on my shoulder and I turned to look at him.

"Are you okay, now?"

"Yeah, I'll be fine. Just remember, I did warn you I couldn't dance. They'll need the patience of saints to teach me."

"You couldn't have two more patient men teaching you and I'm confident, you'll be lighting up the stage for clients in no time. I'll be in my office if you need me."

We all watched as Jake left the stage and I breathed a sigh of relief. Knowing he'd been seated at the bar watching, had unnerved me. It was better that he didn't watch until I no longer made a fool of myself.

"Right, let's get started. I'll hold you in place until you get the knack of staying on the pole," Chris assured me. He was a big man in build with well-defined muscles. He appeared to be more than capable of holding me in place.

I took a closer look at both of the men. Chris was around my height and his muscles bulged but not to the extent of a body builder. Taking into account his fair skin, blonde hair and ice blue eyes, he appeared to have Scandinavian heritage. I guessed he was in his mid-twenties. Pedro was around four inches shorter than the two of us. His name suggested South American heritage and his looks certainly confirmed it. His skin was golden brown, his hair blacker than coal and his eyes were extremely dark with streaks of silver which shimmered under the stage lights. He too was probably in his mid-twenties. Both men were indeed beautiful.

"Thanks, I want to do this, but I have no idea why. The last thing that would have entered my mind when I came here was being a dancer in a strip club. I promise, no more tantrums. I'll give it my best shot."

Pedro smiled. "I hope so. I think you're perfect for the routine the boss has in mind but you've got a steep learning curve in front of you. We'll spend an hour on the pole and then hit the gym where we can teach you more complex acrobatics which you'll need to be able to perform."

Chris nodded. "It's easier to learn the complicated moves on the floor before you try them on the pole, but first we need you confident enough to keep your hold and do basic flips.

I straightened my back, along with my resolve and stepped up to the metal pole. After placing my hands where Pedro had previously instructed, I waited for Chris to move into place behind me and hefted myself onto the cool metal. Without being told, I wrapped my right leg around the pole to keep me in place.

"Let me go, Chris."

Chris released the hold on my waist and stepped back. I stayed put! It was a victory. A small one, but one none the less and I was proud of myself.

***

Over the next hour, the two men taught me how to swing myself around the pole and how to tip myself upside down. Chris kept hold of me with his hands firmly jammed on my waist so I didn't finish up on my head. By the time they called a halt to the practice, I was exhausted and sweating from the sheer effort of taking the full weight of my body with my arms.

Pedro threw me a towel. I noted there was a stack of them folded on the side of the stage. As I rubbed the soft material over first my face, then my body, I inhaled the soft scent of strawberries. They were obviously freshly laundered and placed there for this very purpose.

When Chris and Pedro were done, they threw theirs onto the floor not far from the clean pile and I followed suit. I trailed them down to the bar where Pedro ducked behind and grabbed us each a cold bottle of water. We chatted for a few seconds while we eagerly gulped down the cool liquid. Once the bottles were empty, Pedro tossed them into a barrel behind the bar and we headed through the club to a set of stairs that Chris said led down to their dressing room and gym. The light was dim on the staircase, lit only by floor lighting set into the sides of each step. At the bottom, the men turned to the left and threw open the first door they came to before standing back.

"This is the dressing room we all use. Roan and Jake offered to put in separate rooms for each of us but we all thought it was a waste of money. I mean, we're dancing practically naked for strangers, none of us has an issue with being naked in front of each other," Chris explained.

I nodded before stepping further into the large space and taking a look around. Along the two side walls were glossy white tables with a couple of drawers on each side. Above each one was a mirror with small light globes surrounding it. Some of the tables had various tubes and bottles scattered on top. They reminded me of what I'd seen in some Hollywood movies when actresses were getting ready to go on stage. Chris moved to one about half way down the wall to the right of us.

"This is mine, there are quite a few that aren't used so take your pick. We use them to apply makeup, do our hair, apply glitter on our bodies, that kind of thing." He opened one of the drawers. "I keep my G-strings in here."

Pedro led me to the rear of the huge room, we passed four poles spaced well apart down the center. There was a wall of doors against the back wall and he opened one for me to see inside. "This is where we keep the costumes we wear."

"Oh, I thought we only wore G-strings?"

"No. We usually start off in a costume of some sort and strip down to G-strings during the routine. Most of us wear boots and the costumes could be a police uniform, sailor, soldier and so on. Mine is a fireman's costume."

"So, all different themes."

"It adds interest for the customers and they get excited watching us strip off."

Chris continued. "The slower we are to strip down, the more excited they get and the more money they throw on stage. So, when we get up there, we aren't in a hurry."

"So, getting up there and doing the routine at the speed of light won't bring me much income, huh?" I laughed.

"Your outfits start and finish the same way. There's not really anything you can strip off, being totally naked isn't allowed. You'll see what we mean once the costumes are made. We have a lady a few streets away who sews them for us," Chris informed me before continuing. "We have four waiters who work the room on Friday and Saturday, they're the busiest nights. As you saw when you came in, they wear black pants and black bow ties. We're open all night those two nights but close at one in the morning on the others. Two waiters work the other nights but if it gets busy, we help out. There are two shows – 8pm and 11pm and they each last for an hour. Whoever is performing has a half hour show and then the other dancer or dancers go on. The shows are all very different. We usually throw in a new routine here and there for the regular customers who have seen the same ones over and over."

"Don't the regulars get sick of the same thing?"

"They don't appear to, they keep coming back."

Pedro agreed with Chris. "We have a lot of regulars. Some come in the same night every week while some come in a couple of nights a week and the nights usually vary. There are also businessmen who drop by when they're in town. It's a club district so some men call in when they're done with one of the other clubs."

"Sounds like Jake and Roan are doing pretty good."

Chris nodded. "Very. They have an excellent reputation for keeping drugs and bad seeds out. Johnny, one of our bouncers is a Maori who is originally from New Zealand and the guy is fucking enormous. He knows the streets well and no-one fucks with him. Balati is every bit as big. He's from Samoa and is just as knowledgeable about drug dealers and gangs in the area as Johnny. There's no-one getting through the front doors that they don't want inside. J, as we all call him does Sunday though to Tuesday on his own. Balati does Wednesday and Thursday and they both work Fridays and Saturdays. They change their nights every week so they get the same amount of work. They also look out for us."

"What do you mean?" I asked Chris.

"If a customer gets handsy or refuses to back off, whoever is working will step in and eject them from the club. It's one of the reasons it's safe to work here."

"Sounds good. Why are the poles down here?"

"Warm up poles for before we go on stage. It helps prevent muscle injury. There's two in the gym as well."

"Makes sense."

Pedro took me by the hand. I had a feeling it was how these men were, the contact meant nothing sexual.

"Come on, you have more work to do and then we'll take you for lunch."

I eagerly went with them. For the first time in a very long time, I felt lighter somehow. Almost as if I was finally on a path to being able to forgive myself and carve out a new life.

# Chapter Six

**JAKE**

It had been more than an hour since the three men had passed the office door to head downstairs to the gym. Curiosity about how Lee was coping was killing me and I found myself wondering about him instead of focusing on the figures before me.

I sighed loudly, slammed the journal closed and secured it in a locked drawer in my desk. It was coming up on lunchtime so I knew the men would be close to being finished with training. I rolled down the sleeves of my shirt as I trotted downstairs. When I reached the bottom, I turned toward the gym and stopped in the doorway to watch what was happening.

Chris had Lee gripped around the waist while Pedro had his hands folded over Lees in position on the pole. My newest employee was hanging upside down, sweat dripping from his face and from where I stood, I had the perfect view of the cutest ass I'd ever laid eyes on. My cock danced behind the zipper of my dress pants and I was forced to reposition it to ease the uncomfortable pressure. I shouldn't have bothered because a moment later it had hardened to epic proportions.

I watched as the men released Lee. He pushed himself out to one side, straightened his arms and spread his legs into the splits. It highlighted the size of his package as the G-string was pulled tight over his dick. His muscles bulged with the strain of holding the position for the next few seconds and when Pedro called 'done', Lee dropped to his feet gracefully. He wasn't anything like the man I'd seen earlier struggling to hold himself onto the pole.

As I strode into the gym, I grabbed towels from the pile and handed one to each of the men. Lee's face was red with heat from the effort of what he'd done. Our eyes locked and I smiled.

"Well done, Lee."

He dropped his head shyly. "Thank you."

"He's doing really good, Boss. We came in here to work on the floor but Lee insisted on learning on the pole. I think you're right, he's gonna be a star."

Pedro's words caused Lee to fidget, a habit I'd noticed when he was upset, nervous or embarrassed.

"Have you done gymnastics in your past, Lee?" The fact he appeared so supple had me wondering.

"A little at school but I wasn't as good as Steve so I ditched the class."

One way or the other, I was gonna find out who this Steve was and why Lee had been compared to him for what sounded like most of his life.

"What are you doing now, Chris?" I asked.

"We thought after we showered, we'd take Lee down to Mama's for lunch."

"Sounds like a great idea, mind if I join you?"

"Have we ever?" Chris asked. "How many times have we asked you, but you've said no because your head was buried in your fucking books?"

"They have to be done."

"I know, but you rarely take a break to eat properly," Chris argued. "Don't forget, you've worked all night too."

"I'll try and do better, Dad."

The three men laughed before Lee said, "I'll go across to the motel, shower and dress into something decent. I'll meet you back upstairs in twenty?"

"Sounds good."

Lee started from the room and I couldn't tear my eyes away from the rise and fall of his ass. Once he'd left, Pedro started in on me.

"Boss, don't even think about it. He's a kid for fuck sake. A screwed-up kid, I'm guessing. He doesn't need you, or anyone else here, causing him more heartbreak."

"I hear you, Pedro. I won't do anything to hurt him but I want to help. The kid is running from something and he needs to deal with it before it causes him to do something there's no coming back from."

"You think he'll attempt to take his life?" Chris's tone was incredulous.

"Yeah, I do."

"Why?" Pedro asked.

"Why?"

"Why do you think he's capable of killing himself?"

"Something he said earlier. Come on, hit the showers and I'll meet you upstairs. My shout."

"Of course, it is," Chris laughed as the men headed toward the showers.

I made my way back upstairs to wait.

\*\*\*

I was seated at the bar when Lee strode into the club fifteen minutes later. He'd showered, shaved and looked good enough to eat. He was dressed in jeans and a T-shirt which molded perfectly to every muscle. I licked my lips as he approached.

"The others should be here any minute." I'd no sooner finished speaking than Chris and Pedro emerged from downstairs, also dressed in jeans and T-shirts. I didn't miss the fact, they released each other's hands as soon as they stepped back into the club. I'd have to have a chat with the pair and let them know I had no objection to them being in a relationship as long as it didn't interfere with their work or the club. And, they were to keep fucking, love making, screwing – whatever they wanted to call it, off the premises and in the privacy of one of their homes.

I stood up from the stool at the bar where I'd been sitting drinking a bottle of water while I waited.

"Okay, let's go."

I led the way from the club and held the door open for the men to step outside. The day was warm with bright sunshine and clear blue skies. A perfect day for the beach where I loved to take a walk on my day's off.

We strode down the sidewalk toward Mama's Italian Restaurant – *Bel Morso*, which was about a block away. Lee, beside me, Pedro and Chris behind us. I heard the men talking quietly behind us but Lee and I walked in silence.

A few moments later we arrived at the plain glass door which led into the restaurant. A flip sign read 'open'. I opened the door and waited for the other three men to enter before stepping inside and closing the door behind me. 'Mama' was at the front counter. Her face lit up at the sight of us and she waddled our way. She took Pedro in a bear hug first, followed by Chris and then me. We all grunted as the force of her hugs expressed the air from our lungs.

We'd known Mama since before the club had opened. We'd all been exhausted after spending more than ten hours fitting out the interior of the establishment ready for opening and had been in need of a good feed. One of my dancers had eaten at Mama's before and recommended it. We'd all admitted we loved Italian food so the decision was made. The short, round, elderly Italian woman with grey hair and brown eyes had been extremely welcoming and I'd become enamored with her. I suspected the rest of the men, including my brother, had too. Since then, at least some of us visited for a meal almost every day. It was a wonder the dancers, Roan and I weren't the size of a house with the way she fed us up.

Mama gathered Lee's hands into hers before looking up at me. "Who is this *uomo stupendo*?"

"English, Mama," I corrected.

"Sorry. Who is this gorgeous man?"

Lee answered her himself. "My name is Lee and I started at the club this morning."

Mama nodded and addressed me again.

"He will do very well. Men will have hard dicks over this one."

"Mama!" I chastised.

Lee blushed at her words and heat crept into my face.

To hear an Italian Mama use the word 'dick' was amusing, embarrassing and unusual. But, not for this mama. She was capable of letting fly with a torrent of what I'm sure was foul language in her native tongue when she was unhappy about something.

About a month after we opened, I'd sat Mama down and explained about our club and the dancers. I'd told her our men didn't engage in sex on the premises, but they did strip down to G-Strings and dance for our clients. I'd also explained that some participated in lap dances with chosen customers to earn extra money, but that was their choice. It had been important to me that Mama understood. I'd become extremely fond of her and needed her to accept what we all did.

It hadn't bothered her in the least. She'd waved her hand at me and said, "Eeeh, get over yourself. You think I don't know what kind of 'dancing' goes on in that club of yours? I know you run a decent club, not like the brothels on the other side of town, but I see the men coming and going."

I'd breathed a sigh of relief. On the 15th of August every year since we'd known her and found out that was her birthday, we'd turned up to celebrate with her and showered her with gifts. It had become my favorite day of the year and I'm sure it was Mama's too. We also made a point of celebrating our own birthdays at the establishment.

"Come, sit down."

Mama led us to a table by the window which had two bench seats facing each other. I sat down next to Lee, Chris and Pedro slid onto the seat opposite. While Mama left to get us all our drinks – water, Lee perused the menu. The rest of us didn't need to, we knew the menu word for word. We didn't always choose the same meal though. We had a selection we enjoyed and chose a different one each time we visited.

I watched the men opposite smile at each other, their hands were nowhere in sight and I knew now was as good a time as any to discuss the fact I was aware they were now in a relationship. As soon as the young waiter had placed two jugs of iced water and four glasses on the table and moved away, I grasped the opportunity to speak.

"Chris, Pedro, do you two have something to tell me?"

Both men stared at me, then each other before Chris answered.

"No, why?"

"Do you honestly believe I came down in the last shower?"

They again glanced at each other and I watched with amusement as their faces reddened. Lee sat quietly beside me, probably wondering what I was talking about.

"Chris? Pedro?" I tried again.

Pedro finally looked me in the eyes and said, "I love Chris, Boss."

That statement grabbed Chris's attention and his head snapped around to Pedro.

"What?" he asked.

Pedro swiveled on the seat to face him. "I love you, I have for a while."

Chris was stunned and I decided to speak with Pedro to give the man a moment to gather his thoughts.

"How long has this been going on?"

"Three years."

"You hid it well, I only became aware of it a few months ago."

"Why didn't you say something?"

"Why didn't you two?"

Chris found his tongue. "We love our jobs and didn't want you to fire us."

"Why would I do that? As long as you keep your fucking to the privacy of your own homes, I don't have an issue with it. I would have liked you to trust me enough to talk with me, instead of having me find out on my own."

"Sorry. All we've done is hold hands and sneak a few kisses while we're at work, I give you our word," Pedro said.

"I know. I've seen you a few times and today I saw you holding hands when you came up from downstairs. It was never my intention to make you think a relationship was forbidden."

"Thanks." Chris smiled before turning to Pedro. "I love you too. Will you move in with me?"

Pedro's face lit up. He gathered Chris in his arms, kissed him deeply and gave him a resounding 'yes' in answer to his question.

I glanced at Lee who was watching the men with longing, as if what they had was what he wanted too. I was sure it was what I wanted one day, I just had to find the right man.

Mama appeared with a notepad a moment later and took our orders. Lee had decided on the Shrimp Carbonara while I had the Mushroom Risotto. The happily in love men decided on Pasta Con Pomodoro E Basilico.

Over our meal, we learned a little more about Lee but I suspected there was a great deal in his past he skated over.

# Chapter Seven

**LIAM**

I'd never been a big eater and when I'd left home, I'd made do with small portions of takeaway. I couldn't cook and it was all I could afford. Of course, there was plenty of Chinese food thanks to Mrs. Chin but I hadn't eaten Italian in what felt like forever. The Shrimp Carbonara was to die for and I knew I'd be back. While we ate, I decided to find out more about the men I'd be working for and with.

"Do you have family, Pedro?"

"Yeah, my parents live in Brazil with my two sisters. They didn't share my dream of coming to America."

"How long have you been here?"

"Twelve years, I came here when I was fourteen."

"That's young, have you always been a dancer?"

"No, I wasn't a dancer until I met Roan. He found me beaten up, lying in the gutter outside the club one morning. I'd been in a place down the street, a gay club that's no longer there. I'd had too much to drink and been robbed and beaten up on my way home. Roan took me back to his place and took care of me. He offered me a job as a dancer and the rest is history. I'd been a factory worker until then, earning less than minimum wage for fourteen hours work a day, six days a week. I was well and truly sick to death of the site of milk cartons, I can tell you."

"I'm glad he found you and took care of you. What about you, Chris?"

"I'm the youngest of nine kids. My parents live in a town about an hour from here. There was no work there so, at eighteen, I caught the bus here and started asking around for work. Fortunately, Jake was in a convenience store just down the street and heard me ask. When I was told there was nothing and left the store, Jake offered me a job at the club he was setting up with his brother. I'd never danced in my life, but as I had nothing else and was tired of living on the streets, I accepted. Jake let me stay with him until I had the money to get a place of my own."

I forked up more of my meal and asked Jake about himself.

"I know why you started the club with your brother, Jake. Do you have other family?"

"No, just Roan and our parents who live up in Huntersfield about half an hour from here. Roan and I visit on holidays, on their birthdays and at least once a week on our days off. My dad's a Detective and mom's a Lawyer."

I swallowed down a gasp of shock and continued eating. I glanced up to see Jake studying me carefully.

"What?"

Jake shook his head. "Nothing. What about you? Family?"

"Yeah, but we don't speak or see each other. My parents are alive, I have an older brother and two younger sisters. Before I came here, I was working in a Chinese restaurant and studying Accounting – it didn't work out.

I'd said as much as I was going to and the other men must have sensed I was done, they didn't question me further and I changed the subject.

"Who else dances at the club?"

Jake glanced at Pedro and Chris but when they didn't answer, he spoke.

"All the dancers started at the club before we opened five years ago. Either Roan or I found our men one way or another, but like Chris and Pedro, it's their story to tell. So, we have Sam,

Edyn, Tommy and Dixon. They are all in their early to mid-twenties. Pedro's the eldest and the others let him take charge."

Chris laughed. "We don't have any fucking choice. He sulks when we don't do as he asks."

We joined him in laughing before Jake went on.

"Our table staff, who rotate the days they work, are Joey, Clint, Mason, Alex, Neil and Paul. Trace and Jenkins work the bar. Both work Friday and Saturday nights, the other nights either one or the other is on duty. If they get busy on the nights they're alone, one of the waiters helps. The only other staff are Johnny and Balati who I told you about earlier."

"Wow, you have a lot of staff."

"We're a busy club. We open at four in the afternoon and the first show is at eight as you know. Between opening and the first show, the men drink plenty and spend at the card tables. The club has all the correct licenses and I employ men who are legal."

"Except me."

"You're not twenty-one, Lee?" Pedro raised his eyebrows as he stared at Jake.

"No. I'm not eighteen for another five months."

Chris scowled at Jake. "Boss?"

"I know but I don't want him to get away. I'll make a deal with all three of you because when Roan finds out he's gonna fucking lose it. He's against employing anyone under the age of twenty-one although when we were first starting out, he said he'd allow dancers over the age of eighteen as long as they didn't set foot onto the main floor of the club."

Jake pushed away his empty plate and turned to face me.

"I want you to learn the routines with Chris and Pedro and practice until you perfect them. Until your birthday, you'll work on the books in the office and I warn you now, they're a fucking mess. After you turn eighteen, you'll go on stage. Agreed?"

Jake made a point of asking the two men seated opposite if his plan satisfied them. Both nodded in agreement so now it was up to me. And, Roan.

"I agree. If you're dad's a Detective, the last thing you want to do is get on the wrong side of the law."

Mama approached the table and asked if there was anything else we'd like.

"No, Mama, it's time we got back to the club," Jake answered.

We all stood and I waited while Mama hugged the other men. When I started to step away, I was dragged into her arms and hugged so hard, I thought the food would find its way back out of my stomach. Fortunately, for both of us, it didn't.

Jake insisted on paying the check and with bellies full, we started back to the club. When we reached there, Jake instructed Pedro and Chris to help with setting up the club until their food was settled. I was taken through to his office, asked to sit behind the desk and had a bevy of books plonked in front of me.

"I'll get you a coffee and leave you alone for a couple of hours and then you can go back downstairs and practice on the pole."

I nodded and as I opened the first book, Jake slipped from the office and quietly closed the door.

***

Two hours later, I was on my fourth coffee and had done fuck all to get any kind of order into the books. It would take me every bit of the next five months to bring them to a point where their accountant could make sense of the numbers. I can imagine he must have been pulling his hair out when doing their last lot of taxes. There were currently nine months of figures to wade through and straighten out.

I sighed heavily, placed the empty mug back on the desk and picked up the pencil I'd set down beside the book I was working on. I glanced up when the door opened. Jake hovered, seemingly unsure of whether to enter or not.

"Come on in." I spoke on a sigh and placed the pencil back down.

Jake stepped in, closed the door and sat down in the chair I'd been in earlier that morning.

"That bad, huh?"

"How has your accountant not throttled you?"

"He does a lot of screaming and shouting."

"I can imagine. I want you to pick up another couple of ledgers and I'll transcribe the figures correctly into them."

"Isn't it against the law to have two sets of books?"

"No, as long as they both show the same bottom line. We'll keep this set and provide them along with the new ones. That shows you're not hiding anything."

"Okay, I'll pick them up."

"Wait until we're out on Monday. These are the wrong books, I'll make sure you have the right ones."

"Did you learn how to do this from Mrs. Chin?"

"Some of it, the rest I learned in college, even though I was only there for six months."

"If I pay you extra, will you do them for us?"

"As well as dancing?"

"How about you dance Thursdays, Fridays and Saturdays. Take Sundays and Mondays off and do the books on Tuesdays and Wednesdays?"

It sounded like a fucking good deal to me. "Okay but if the dancing fails, I work Monday thru Friday."

"Deal, but the dancing *will* work out. I have some paperwork I need you to fill in, can we do it now?"

I nodded and closed the books while Jake stood, crossed to the filing cabinet and pulled a folder from one of the drawers. He placed a set of employment forms before me and I filled them in. He perused them when I handed them back to him, lifted his head and cocked an eyebrow at me.

"I understand why you don't have an address, but I need a next of kin to contact in case of an emergency."

"You don't need to contact anyone, I'll take care of myself."

"Lee, I need to know. It could be a deal breaker."

I shrugged and stood. "Thanks, anyway. I guess I'll have to find something else."

"They'll want to know before they employ you."

"Not everyone does, it depends on the job. Mrs. Chin didn't ask."

I moved toward the door to leave. Jake stood, reached out and grabbed me by the arm.

"Is it really such a big deal that we know who to call if something happens?"

I locked eyes with his. "Yeah, it is."

Jake sighed and released me.

"Thanks, Jake."

"You can stay. I'll put myself down as next of kin. I don't like it but I'll do it."

"Up to you."

"Go downstairs, Pedro and Chris are waiting for you."

It was obvious Jake was pissed so I left the office without another word and headed downstairs to the dressing room. Once there, I changed into one of the half dozen G-Strings I'd been given and found Pedro and Chris in the gym.

***

"That's it. Now, wrap your right leg around the pole and use the back of your knee and top of the calf muscle to grip it," Pedro instructed.

Chris was holding me tightly which was fortunate because after a couple of hours of supporting my weight while performing acrobatic tricks – simple though they were, every muscle in my body was screaming at me. Sweat trickled from my soaked hair into my eyes and no matter how much resin I applied to my hands, they still slipped on the pole.

"Release your grip, arch your back and drop your head and arms toward the floor."

"Fuck." My leg was also beginning to slide from the dampness.

"It's okay, let go. Chris will guide you into position and I'll keep your leg in place."

I released the pole and felt my leg slip a fraction before Pedro secured it in place with a vice like hold. Chris held my hands with one of his and eased my back into an arch. At the same time, he kept my head between my arms and lowered me until my fingertips almost brushed the floor and I was being held by only my knee – and Pedro.

Chris made sure I was steady and released me. I held the position, but when Pedro released my leg, I started to slide. Chris rushed in and caught me in his arms before we both ended up on the floor with me in his lap. We all dissolved into fits of laughter and Pedro decided we'd had enough for the day. It was time to shower and get back upstairs.

I thanked both of the men and pushed to my feet, when I turned to leave the room, my eyes locked on Jake in the doorway. His expression was one of anger, almost fury. Surely, he couldn't still be pissed about the conversation we'd had upstairs?

# Chapter Eight

**JAKE**

I'd heard the men laughing when I reached the bottom of the stairs and as I stepped into the doorway of the gym it was to find Lee seated in Chris's lap on the floor. I felt my blood boil instantly at the sight. Problem was, the more I tried to figure out why the scene angered me, the more pissed I became. I mean, it wasn't as if I had a claim on the young man. I'd already decided he was out of bounds. The concern in his eyes, when he finally noticed me, had my anger fizzling and I moved into the room.

"Something I should know about?" I attempted to lighten my mood.

Pedro shook his head. "You should have been here a couple of minutes ago."

"What happened?" I asked.

"Chris dived for Lee as he slid from the pole and they both ended up on the floor in a heap." Pedro burst into laughter. "I wish you could have seen your face, Chris when you thought Lee was going to land on his head. You're gonna have to teach us that move of yours, it was worthy of any ballerina."

I laughed at the images Pedro had put in my head. "You two ready for tonight?"

Pedro slammed his hands on his waist and threw one leg out to the side. "When haven't we been ready?"

"The night Tommy fell down the steps and you two went with him to hospital. A hospital which is ten minutes away and it took you almost two hours to go there and back. I had to send Edyn and Sam on in your places for the eight o'clock show and you had to perform the eleven o'clock. Knowing what I know now, I wouldn't find it hard to believe you took a detour to have a fuck."

"That's not fair, we got caught up in traffic."

I nodded. "Hmm, why do I find that hard to believe?"

Chris and Pedro pouted and I burst into laughter again.

"Go and do whatever you do at this time in the evening. Lee, can I have a word?"

I chuckled as I watched the two men flounce off.

Lee waited for me to speak, he appeared apprehensive. Sweat droplets trickled over his muscles, his G-string was soaked and hid nothing. My dick showed a great deal of interest. I tore my eyes away from the bulge and focused on what I wanted to ask the young man.

"Are you staying to watch the performances tonight, or are you going to call it a day."

"I'm fucked but I'd like to watch the guys on stage. Do Pedro and Chris always start so early in the morning?" I wasn't sure I had the stamina to keep up a pace like todays.

"No, the dancers usually come in around four. They're performing a new routine tonight and came in early to get extra practice in. The other dancers will be in any time now. The bar staff and wait staff come in around three and start getting the club ready for when we open. They're all working upstairs now."

"Aren't you tired after working all last night and being up all day?"

"Yeah, but I wanted to find out what plans you had before I grab a couple of hours on the couch in my office. I'm used to functioning on next to no sleep every second weekend, Roan's the same."

"I'm going to shower and go back to the motel for a couple of hours sleep. I'll be back in time for tonight's shows."

"What about dinner?"

"Haven't even given it a thought."

"How about I pick something up when I grab dinner for the other men? I usually grab a bunch of burgers."

"Sounds perfect. I'll be back around six thirty."

"Okay. See you then and thanks for today."

"Thank you, Jake."

I walked Lee out and while he headed for the shower, I dragged my tired body back to the office.

***

Loud knocking on the office door jolted me awake. I glanced at the clock on the wall to see it was almost 6 pm. I'd been out like a light the moment I'd hit the couch and hadn't heard a thing until now. The door was locked so whoever was knocking would have to wait until I dragged my sleep fogged body onto my feet.

"Give me a minute," I shouted.

I sat up and scrubbed my hands over my face in an attempt to wake up. Pushing onto my feet, I crossed to the door, unlocked it and opened it to find Mason, one of our waiters.

"Joey told me to wake you up at six." He turned to leave.

"Has he gone home?"

Mason turned back to face me. "Yeah, about an hour ago."

I nodded and he left. I crossed the floor to a small closet where I kept a couple of changes of clothes for when I worked the Friday and Saturday shift. I often didn't go home until late on the Sunday night. Roan was the same when he worked the weekend.

I grabbed fresh clothes, a towel and my toiletries bag, closed the door to the closet and turned to leave the room. Lee, who was leaning against the door frame watching me, smirked.

"What are you smirking at?" My voice was gruff and husky from sleep.

"You look like shit."

I dragged my fingers through my hair and when I reached the door, Lee stood aside so I could pass him.

"Fuck off."

"Whoa, we're grumpy when we wake up, I'll have to remember that."

I gave him the finger as I strode off to have a shower.

"I'll be with Pedro and Chris. Find your happy face while you're gone."

I again gave Lee the finger and heard him laugh at the gesture. As I descended the steps, I thought about how comfortable the young man seemed to be. It was unusual for someone in a new job to be so relaxed and comfortable. He appeared to be happy and confident for one so young. It had me wondering about what had happened in his life to put the sadness and pain in his eyes. Even when he was joking and smiling, the happiness never quite reached his eyes.

I stepped into an empty shower stall, placed my clothes on a shelf and removed the soap, razor, shampoo and conditioner from my bag. I flicked on the water and allowed it to heat while I stripped off. I relaxed under the spray of hot water, it was soothing to my tired, aching muscles. I washed, shaved, flicked off the faucet and stepped into the dry section of the cubicle to dry off. I felt a whole heap better but wanted to crawl into a soft bed and sleep for twelve hours. It was the same every weekend. The long hours took their toll on both me and my brother. I wondered whether it would be better if we employed a manager to share the all-nighters. I'd have to sit down and discuss it when I caught up with Roan in the next day or so.

Once showered, fully awake and in a better frame of mind, I grabbed my belongings and headed to the dressing room where the dancers usually were at this time of night. Pedro and Chris were both working the poles and talking to each other about parts of the new routine they were going to be performing in the eight o'clock show. Lee was laughing about something with Dixon and Sam. I paused for a moment and studied him. Fuck he was gorgeous. I reminded myself again, he was not for me.

Sam spotted me first and started toward me.

"Hi, Boss."

"Sam, everything okay?"

"Yep, no problem with any of us. I've been talking with Lee. I like him, he'll fit in well."

I'd barely heard Sam's words. Lee had glanced my way and his eyes locked with mine. It was as if everything else, except the two of us, had vanished. I climbed back out of my head to find Sam staring at me.

"You left me for a minute there," Sam said.

"Yeah, sorry. Well, I'll leave you to it. I'm going to get something to eat for all of us."

"It's burger night!" Dixon fist pumped the air and the others laughed.

Roan and I always provided the meal at night for all of the workers at the club. The takeaway varied from one night to the next – Italian, Chinese, Thai – you get the idea. Tonight, as Dixon said, was burger night.

"I'll be back in fifteen."

We had a standing order for Saturday nights and it was picked up around 6.30 every week. I'd called earlier to add an extra burger and fries for Lee. I started to leave the room when Lee jogged over.

"I'll come with you, give you a hand."

"Thanks. I'm capable of carrying it on my own but I'd appreciate the company."

I stood back so he could pass me and followed his cute ass back upstairs. It was going to be painful having him working here and knowing he couldn't be mine. And, he couldn't. The age difference was only one of the barriers holding me back.

\*\*\*

The air was warm, balmy, when we stepped from the air-conditioned club.

"This way." I laid a hand on Lee's arm and guided him to the left.

We strode down the sidewalk, weaving in and out of the large number of people headed in the opposite direction. *The Better Burger* was busy and I had to push past the crowd to reach the counter.

"Yo, Gary! Jake's here," Betty shouted to a vacant window behind her. Within seconds, two large brown paper bags were placed on the window ledge. Betty grabbed them and handed them over to me.

She cocked her head in Lee's direction and asked, "New dancer?"

"Yep. Betty meet Lee."

Betty thrust an arm over the glass topped counter and shook Lee's hand. "Pleased to meet you, Lee." She winked at me. "Cute."

I laughed before saying goodnight and handing a bag over to Lee. We pushed our way back out of the store and onto the street.

"Looks like business is good," Lee commented.

"This time of year is always busy. The warm weather brings people out."

We hurried back to the club and I signaled the men on the way in to let them know food was on. Half followed us to my office and grabbed their food before heading to a small staff room which was located beside the bar. The other half would keep an eye on the floor and serve customers.

Paul also grabbed a meal for Trace at the bar. They often ate together on the nights they both worked while one of the floor staff manned the bar. I wondered if theirs was another relationship I was unaware of. Once the first shift of men had eaten, they would swap places. There was a microwave in the staff room for the men to heat food but the burger shop always wrapped our food in silver foil which seemed to keep it hot for a long time.

"I'll go and let the dancers know the food's here. You start," I said to Lee.

He headed for the door. "I'll go, back in a few."

Before I could respond, he was out the door. I dropped into the chair behind my desk and pulled out the burger meal with my name on it. Every Saturday I worked, I broke my habit of eating healthy for a satay chicken burger. Boring I know, but it was just so damn good. My mouth watered as I tore away the foil and unwrapped the inner paper. Steam wafted from it and delicious scents floated in the air. I then opened a package of fries which were covered in a mixture of spices and popped one in my mouth. Closing my eyes, I hummed and savored the burst of flavor which hit my tongue.

"Can we interrupt?" Pedro spoke cheekily as the dancers entered my office and pulled out their meals.

Lee stood back and waited. Once they'd finished and left to head back downstairs, Lee reached for the last remaining meal.

"I got you an Italian burger and fries, I wasn't sure what you'd like and I'd forgotten to ask before you left this afternoon. You seemed to enjoy the food from Mamas so I took a chance."

Lee sat in the chair opposite and unwrapped his food. "Italian....burger?"

"Yeah. Beef with a slice of mozzarella cheese and Bolognese sauce."

"Sounds good." Lee tore the rest of the wrapping away, lifted it to his mouth and bit into the bun.

Spaghetti sauce dripped onto his chin and although I was tempted to spring from my chair and lick it away, I handed him a napkin instead. He nodded in thanks as he chewed the mouthful and swallowed. "This is good. I think this will be my new favorite takeaway."

"I know what you mean, we all love burger night." I took a large bite of my chicken and almost moaned again.

"What's yours?"

"Chicken Satay."

"Sounds tasty."

"It is. I've tried the others but for the past six months, it's been this one for me. It's just so damn good."

Lee laughed before getting stuck into his food. We ate in silence until the burgers were finished and only fries remained. I decided to see if Lee would open up to me.

"Tell me about your past, Lee. What is it that caused you to sever ties with your family?"

"It's a long story and you'd kick me out of here if I told you. I wouldn't blame you either."

"Why? I don't understand. What could be so bad that you'd think I'd turn my back on you?"

Lee sighed, pushed the uneaten fries away and toyed with the sticker on the bottle of water before lifting his eyes to mine.

"Jake, I really need this job, please don't push me on this."

I wasn't happy to let it go but something in my head was screaming at me not to push the issue. He'd already run once to get here, he could run again and I knew I wouldn't be able to live with myself if he did something desperate.

"I won't but please, come and talk to me when you're ready. Please don't do something to harm yourself."

Lee nodded but didn't give me an answer. I felt an ominous feeling of dread drop over me.

Before I could say anything else, Pedro appeared in the doorway.

"Lee, we're about to get ready. Do you want to come and watch how we apply makeup and warm up?

Lee pushed back in the chair and jumped to his feet. He appeared anxious to escape me and disappointment settled deep in my belly.

"Catch you later, Jake. Thanks for the burger."

With those few words, Lee was out the door.

# Chapter Nine

**LIAM**

I headed downstairs, concern weighed heavily on my shoulders. Jake was becoming more insistent about my past and I knew, without a doubt, he'd regard me with disgust when he found out the terrible thing I'd done. Tears pricked the back of my eyes. For the first time in my life, I felt like I'd found somewhere I truly belonged. I was sure we would become good friends if I was given a chance.

As I descended the stairs, I made the decision to take things one day at a time. Hopefully, Jake would let it go. So, why did I get the feeling, he wouldn't?

Pedro and Chris were at their dressing tables when I entered the room. Sam and Dixon were nowhere to be seen. They had plenty of time before their eleven and eleven-thirty shows. Edyn who had the eight-thirty was in the gym, Pedro informed me.

I headed to where Pedro sat. He was wearing only a bright orange, sparkly G-string. When I glanced toward Chris, I noted he was wearing one in blue. I dragged a chair from the table beside Pedro and sat down.

"So, what's the new routine?"

Pedro shook his head. "No, like everyone else, you have to wait and see."

"Okay. So, makeup. What do we wear?"

"It depends on the routine but the basics are always the same. Foundation, powder, blush to highlight the cheekbones, eyeliner in a color to match the routine."

"What do you mean?" I interrupted.

"Black or brown for smoky, come to me, eyes. As a fireman, I wear red for danger eyes. It's personal choice really. You won't need eye makeup, you'll be wearing masks for your routines. We wear false lashes with black mascara and whichever color eyeshadow we think works. We want to make the eyes pop. Either as sensuous, excited, mysterious, that kind of thing. All our makeup is applied with a heavy hand or it doesn't show up under the stage lights and we look washed out, half-dead."

"Oooh, you're a long way from half-dead in the bedroom, gorgeous," Chris cooed.

Pedro and I laughed while Chris blew his lover a kiss.

"Getting back to serious business....." Pedro frowned at Chris who replied by blowing another kiss. "We use oil-soaked glitter on our bodies and there are two reasons for this. One, it makes our body's shimmer under the lights and two, if some asshole gropes us, they slide right off."

"Do you get groped very often?"

Chris answered. "Not if they know what's good for them. Balati or Johnny are always close by and the men find themselves ejected - permanently."

"That makes me feel a little better."

"You don't have to worry about anyone in here. Most of the men are real gentlemen and they respect our boundaries. The club is safe for both us and the clients," Pedro assured me.

The men were finished applying their makeup and I watched as they styled their hair and coated their bodies with the glittery gel. When they both stood and turned toward me, envy shot through me. They were stunning. I'd never live up to the standard they set.

I watched as they applied gel to their asses and then they took turns applying it to each other's backs.

"Time to get dressed," Pedro smiled before heading to where the costumes were stored at the back of the room.

"Time for you to head upstairs, Lee. The others have been banned from seeing before we go on stage, the same applies to you."

"Oh, okay. Um, have a good show, break a leg, whatever is good luck for you."

The men laughed at my uncertainty.

"Good luck is fine," Chris answered.

Pedro shooed me with his hands. I got the message, left the room and headed upstairs to find Jake.

***

I found Jake leaning against the bar, keeping an eye on things. The club was packed, it seemed there was standing room only. I wandered over and climbed onto a stool next to him. A tall man, with skin the color of ebony, finished up with the customer he'd been serving and came over to me. Like everyone else here, the man was beautiful. His eyes were the color of molten chocolate, not a blemish marred his skin. His pouty lips were naturally pink and black curly hair framed his face.

"You're the new boy, Jake told me about. I'm Jenkins, very pleased to meet you."

114

"Yeah, I'm Lee." I shook hands with the man.

"What would you like?"

"Just water, thanks."

"What is it with you lot, a drink now and then wouldn't hurt."

Jake swiveled to face Jenkins and spoke quietly. "Underage, Jenkins. *Very* underage."

"Oh, should he even be in here?"

"No, but I'll let him watch the performance this once."

Jenkins slid a bottle of water toward me. "Thanks." I unscrewed the cap and took a large gulp before turning my eyes toward the stage.

The lights had been turned down low in the main area of the club but were left bright over the stage. A hush fell over the room and men gravitated closer to the stage. A voice came over the loudspeaker. It was Jake's, obviously recorded.

"Please make welcome, for your pleasure and enjoyment....Pedro and Sam. Tonight they have a brand new routine so sit back and remember the rules."

Music blared, a deep beat caused the floor beneath my feet to vibrate and the two men erupted on stage. I felt my mouth drop open at the sight and every drop of saliva evaporated.

Pedro wore a pair of brown street pants and a white shirt with the top three or four buttons left unfastened. Across his eyes he wore a bright orange sparkly mask, in his hand was a large sack with a black dollar sign painted on it. Chris was dressed as a policeman. He wore blue pants, a blue shirt and like Pedro, the top was left open, revealing his well-muscled chest. He wore a police hat on his head and carried a truncheon.

Pedro raced around the stage, Chris in hot pursuit, waving the truncheon. A chase ensued, amazing acrobatics including leaping over each other, were performed. The sack was thrown off to one side before Pedro leapt onto one of the poles and began twisting and turning. His moves hypnotic. Chris slid the truncheon off to the side of the stage and his hat followed close behind. He seemed to float through the air and landed on the pole above Pedro.

Together, they performed a sensuous routine. Limbs tangled. They kissed and seemed to defy gravity with their moves. Clients in the club were spellbound. Holding each other, they slid back to the floor and proceeded to remove each other's clothing until Pedro was wearing only the bright orange G-string and Chris wore blue.

They sashayed to the front of the stage, hips swinging, and numerous men surged forward. Being a Saturday night, both Johnny and Balati were on duty and stood on the floor to each side of the stage, watching for anyone who might become a threat to the dancers.

The men took one side of the stage each, spread their feet and swinging their hips, lowered to the floor and back into a standing position. Money was tossed onto the floor near them and some was stuffed into the flimsy G-strings. It lasted for only a few minutes but by the time the men returned to a pole of their own, money littered the stage. Even from where I sat, I saw more than one bill was a hundred dollar note.

I watched mesmerized by the array of tricks they performed and when the performance ended, I clapped loudly, along with everyone else. The men in the club remained where they were, awaiting the next dancer.

Jake turned to face me. "What did you think?"

"I'm in deep shit. There's no way I could be that good."

Jake laughed. "If what I saw today is any indication, you'll be even better. None of the other men picked up the basic moves as fast as you have. You're gonna be a star. I have no doubt."

"We'll see." I climbed from the stool and stood before Jake. "I'm going to the motel to get some sleep unless you want me to stay."

"No, I think you've earned your money today. I'll pick you up on Monday morning. Ten o'clock okay?"

I frowned before realization dawned. "The apartment, of course. Don't you want me in tomorrow?"

"Nope, Sunday and Monday are your days off, remember."

"Okay, I'll see you on Monday then. Thanks, Jake, for everything."

"Pleasure. If you need me before Monday, call me."

I nodded but knew I wouldn't be calling him. Dealing with the man my body seemed to be attracted to was hard enough at work. No, I needed to keep reminding myself, Jake was my boss, not my boyfriend. I just hoped my body would get onboard with the fact.

After waving toward Jenkins and Trace, who were busy with customers, I left the club and loped across the street to the motel. I let myself into the room and headed straight for the shower. After drying off, I collapsed into bed, naked. I didn't bother with the porn channel, I was way too exhausted to jack off. Or, so I thought.

As I lay with my eyes closed in the darkness, visions of Jake filled my mind. A naked Jake! My hand reached for my already stiff cock and I stroked languidly as more and more images flashed behind my eyes. Images of me kissing Jake. Kneeling in front of him, my hands on his sumptuous ass while taking his cock into my mouth and sucking him to the back of my throat. My fingers pushing through the tightness of his hole and sinking deep into his warmth.

I slid my hand over the length of my dick. Faster. Harder. I threw back the covers and writhed in pleasure while envisaging my dick buried deep in Jake's ass. A kaleidoscope of color flashed behind my eyes as I shouted Jake's name and succumbed to a powerful orgasm. An orgasm which held me in its grip longer than any before it. When my pounding heart rate finally slowed and my body stopped trembling, I pulled the covers back over me and rolled onto my side. I'd told Jake I was in deep shit. I certainly was. In more ways than one. The last thing I should be doing was falling for my boss.

***

Sunday passed with the speed of a snail on crutches. I spent the day getting to know the area, window shopping – it's safer that way, especially when you don't have spare money to blow on something which isn't a matter of life or death in the need department. I'd also checked out a few real estate advertisements in both the local newspaper and online. There were a few which were worse than what I'd left behind and a few that were a little out of my reach. If I made plenty in tips, I'd be able to manage easily, but that wouldn't even be on the radar for another five months. I guessed I could take a place which was affordable for now and move into a better place once I started dancing.

I sighed heavily as I pushed the door to my motel room open and stepped inside. Before closing the door, I gazed across the street where the pink neon lights spelling out *Velvet Post* had already come to life. It was just on dusk and the lights would glow brightly once darkness fell. I was tempted to cross the road and spend more time with the object of my attraction. I'd already jerked off three times while images of him ravishing me played like a movie in my mind. Who the fuck was I kidding? One day. One fucking day I'd known the man and I had a crush the size of the Empire State Building. No, I'd stay put in the motel. I needed to give my libido a chance to cool off.

I threw the key down onto a small desk, kicked off my shoes and flopped down on the bed. It was barely six o'clock but I'd had a big lunch at a Turkish place uptown and had no desire for a meal. I was tired, but not worn out. I felt hyper. My skin crawled like a thousand ants had invaded just beneath the surface. It was what happened whenever I became anxious. I shook my head, grabbed the remote control and turned on the television. When the screen flashed into life and a couple going at it were revealed, I switched it back off. I wasn't in the mood to watch people fucking each other.

I jumped back to my feet and padded across the room to a small refrigerator where I'd stashed a few bottles of water when I'd arrived. I removed one, twisted off the cap and stood at the window, gazing out onto the street. Was I hoping to catch a glimpse of him? I was going fucking crazy, turning into some kind of deranged stalker. Then, I remembered, he wasn't even there. Roan was on duty. I pulled the curtains closed, instantly plunging the room into darkness and after setting the bottle on the bedside table, I stripped off and lay on the bed. The night was warm, the air conditioner broken so there was no need for covers. My dick lay flaccid against my thigh. Until I closed my eyes and Jake materialized in my thoughts.

I rolled onto my belly, trapping my dick beneath me and kept my hands under the pillow which supported my head. There was no way I was going to succumb every time his face appeared before my eyes. If I did, one of two things – or both, would happen. Either my dick would end up red raw, swollen and painful from being tugged at and/or I was gonna be sporting a boner every time I clapped eyes on the man. Nope, it stopped. Right now!

# Chapter Ten

**JAKE**

**M**y skin tingled in anticipation as I crossed the street to Liam's motel room. I'd advised Roan I'd be at the club around two. As expected, he'd exploded when I'd confessed the young man's age but when I'd told him of my plan to keep him in the office until after he turned eighteen, he'd reluctantly agreed. I think being informed that the hated books were to be taken care of went a long way toward swaying him to agree with me. He had insisted that Liam was not to be on the floor for any reason during club opening times. I'd promised my brother faithfully; our newest dancer would not step foot from the office when we were trading.

I'd missed Lee the previous day and had found I couldn't concentrate on a damn thing. No matter how many times I told myself he was off limits, it appeared my body was refusing the command and I found myself wanting to be with him. My dick had been so hard all day, it was downright painful and I'd had to remedy the problem in the privacy of my locked office – twice! It hadn't made a scrap of difference. The moment he popped into my head again, my dick responded by coming to attention. Maybe I'd made a mistake in hiring the gorgeous young man. My brain said yes. My body said no.

I shook my head as I approached an orange painted door with a brass number five attached to it. I raised my hand to knock but the door swung open and Liam stood before me. He was dressed in tight blue jeans which appeared to have been painted on and had paired them with a pale gray Henley. I found myself wanting to fuck him into next week. Did I mention the guy was drop-dead gorgeous?

"Hi," I murmured. "Did you have a good day off?"

I waited while Liam closed and locked the door.

"Quiet. I took advantage of the time to have a look around town, find out where everything is. You?"

"I hung around at work and tried to get something done on the books. I was too distracted and didn't make much progress." *By you.*

"I wouldn't worry about them. Leave the takings receipts in the drawer and I'll sort it out. Where to first? I found a couple of Estate offices up in town, will we check those out?"

"We can, but first I want to show you a building where all the other dancers have apartments. It's gated, so pretty secure and only a ten-minute walk from here. The complex has an indoor pool, tennis court and gym. I think you'll like it and you won't be coming home late at night on your own."

"Sounds good if I can afford the rent. Lead the way."

We weaved our way through people on the sidewalk who were distracted with talking on their phones and not watching where they were walking. Others stood on the edge of the gutter with unfolded maps and were arguing about which direction they should take.

I drew to a stop in front of a pair of iron gates which were supported on each side by large stone pillars. On the right side was a small gate where people on foot could enter without opening the larger gates. They were more suited to giving vehicles entry to the property. A sign announcing the name of the complex in gold lettering– *Harborside Apartments* – was attached on the left side. Underneath this was a push button panel where the code for access was entered. I punched in the numbers and soundlessly, the gate swung open. We stepped through and came to a stop so Liam could take in the surroundings.

The building, off to our right, comprised three floors with each apartment having two bedrooms and an open plan living area. The gardens were practical and well-maintained. The views over the harbor were stunning, especially on a bright sunny day like today. Boats of every type bobbed on the sparkling water. Colorful masts contrasted against the rich blue of the sky. On the harbor-front of the complex were barbecue grills, wooden benches and tables. On a day like today, it was a wonderful place to sit and contemplate the ways of the world. *Or Lee.* To our left was the tennis court and a building which housed the pool and gym. It was a great place to live especially for those who were single.

"I can't afford this, Jake."

"You don't know that. Come and have a look. It's apartment number 312. Third floor with great views."

I shrugged. "I guess I can dream. Lead the way."

We crossed to a glass door, I punched in the code and the door swung open. When we stepped inside, the air was pleasantly cool.

"There's an elevator or you can take the stairs."

"Stairs. If I'm to be your dancer, I need to get fit."

I raked my eyes over Liam's firm, very well put together body and shook my head.

"There's not a damn thing wrong with your body."

"Thanks, but after an hour of training with Chris and Pedro, I know I don't have anywhere near the strength or stamina I need. I asked Pedro what I could do to strengthen my body and he suggested Tommy and gave me his number. I called and asked if he'd work out a training routine I can use in the gym. We're having coffee later and he'll talk me through what he thinks will suit me."

*Why do I have the sudden urge to rip Tommy's arms from his body?* "That sounds good. From what I know of Pedro and Chris's routines, they require a lot of upper body strength."

"Do they do all the choreography?"

"Yes. The other guys add in their own moves here and there but it's mostly Pedro and Chris who work out the routines. They're fucking good at it too. I can't wait to see these 'spectacular' routines they've been going on about for the past couple of months. I've seen bits and pieces but not the entire dance."

"To be honest, I'm surprised they were happy to teach me. It seems the dances are special to them and they're trusting me – someone who's never danced in his life, to do them justice."

I stopped at the door to the apartment and turned to face Lee.

"I think you will."

"How do you know? You saw what I was like on Saturday."

"No…. I saw how you started on Saturday and what you were doing by the time you finished. You were incredible and I really believe, I have discovered a star."

Lee laughed. "Yeah, right. You go on believing that and you might be sorely disappointed. Steve's the star, not me. Now, show me this apartment."

Lee pushed past me and headed inside, leaving me to wonder again. Who the fuck was this Steve and why did I feel inclined to strangle the man? As I stepped through the door, Lee attempted to push past me to leave. I placed my hands on his arms. Big mistake! Fucking huge mistake! Electricity surged through my body like I'd touched a live wire. I hurriedly pulled my hands back and when I gazed into Lee's eyes, I could see the confusion. Had he felt it too? It took me a moment to find my voice.

"Where are you going?"

"Have you seen this place? I can't afford this."

"Yes, you can. The others manage well and you'll be earning around the same as them. Please, at least have a look around."

Lee shrugged and stepped back, allowing me to enter. I closed the door behind me and watched as he crossed to the huge wall of glass which had a breathtaking view of the harbor below. I stepped up beside him, careful to keep enough distance between us to prevent another over the top reaction by my treacherous body.

"What do you think?" I asked quietly.

Liam turned slightly to face me. "This place is amazing. I just wish I really could afford it."

He turned toward the large living area and while he studied it. I remained quiet. The apartment was furnished with two leather sofas in bright red. Plump white cushions were piled over them. A black and white, highly polished coffee table was positioned between them. On the wall was a large flat screen television and beneath it was a black and white entertainment center. The dining table was also black and white with six red leather chairs. A matching cabinet for dishes and flatware stood against one wall. The kitchen was also black and white, punctuated with red appliances and canisters.

"I love it," Lee murmured, with such longing in his voice, it shocked me.

"Come and have a look at the bedrooms."

I strode to a small hallway and through the first door off to my right. In the center of the room stood a king-sized bed decorated in black, white and red with scatter cushions in matching colors. Two black and white bedside tables held white based lamps with black shades. A large white chest of drawers stood in the center of two doors. I threw the first one open.

"This is the walk-in closet." I moved to the other door. "This is the ensuite. There's another identical bedroom for overnight guests across the hall, it also has a walk-in closet and ensuite. At the end of the hall there's a toilet with a small vanity for visitors."

I stood back while Lee studied the huge bathroom. The walk-in shower had multiple jets from the floor to the ceiling and acted like a water massage to soothe aching muscles. Two black porcelain basins rested atop a white vanity cupboard. The bath had numerous jets for those who preferred to sit down and experience their relaxing effect. A white porcelain toilet and matching bidet were positioned on the wall opposite. Like the living area, the bedroom and bathroom had a full wall of glass. The view was that of the city.

Lee hurried back to the living area and I caught up with him at the door. Again, I placed a hand on his arm and felt the tantalizing zap of attraction.

"Lee, what's wrong?"

"I love it but I don't know how the others afford it."

"How much do you think it is?"

"I have no idea, I don't know the area, but I do know it's not for me. People like me don't deserve to live in a place like this."

I spun him to face me. He stared at me with so much sadness in his eyes. "Lee, please talk to me. Let me help."

I watched as tears sprang to his eyes. "Thanks, Jake, but there's nothing anyone can do."

I tightened my grip before he moved away. "It's six hundred and fifty dollars a month."

Lee gave me a look of incredulity, as if I'd lost my ever-loving mind. "No way."

I nodded. "Yep. Would you like me to take you down to meet Angus, the agent? He's a friend of mine."

Lee studied me for a moment before nodding. "Thank you."

I released his arm and followed him through the door, locking it after us.

***

I held the door open for Lee to step inside the office and followed behind. Sarah was seated at the reception desk and glanced up when we entered.

"Jake, Hi. You here to see Angus?"

"Yeah, he's expecting us." I turned toward Lee. "This is Lee."

Sarah smiled widely, stretched out her hand and the two shook.

"He's a new dancer at the club."

The woman visibly deflated at my words. I guess she'd hoped the handsome man was someone she could get together with.

"I'll get Angus."

"Did I hear someone mention my name?"

I turned, shook hands with one of my oldest and dearest friends, clapping him on the back. He stepped past me when he noticed Lee and the way his eyes lit up had me wanting to throttle him. Yeah, Angus was gay and since college, we'd gotten together now and again. We enjoyed spending time in each other's company but couldn't seem to take our friendship to the next level, despite being great together in bed.

Both of us had admitted, something was missing. We loved each other but as friends, nothing more.

"This is Lee, a new dancer at the club. We came down so he can sign the lease on Apartment 312 at *Harborside*."

Angus clutched Lee's hand for a little too long and anger laced jealousy surged through me. There was no doubting, the two men were equally beautiful. Angus was taller than me by a couple of inches and he didn't carry an ounce of fat on his well worked body. His skin was creamy white – a testament to his Scottish heritage and his eyes were ice blue. I knew his long, shaggy hair was silky soft, my fingers had tangled in it often enough. He wore it tied back in a ponytail. Dressed in a business suit, the man was extremely sexy and appealing.

"Jake?"

"Yes," I answered Angus.

"I asked if you'd liked to come through to the office with us while I get Lee to sign the paperwork."

"Sorry, checked out there for a minute. I have a lot of things on my mind." Lee not being mine was one of them.

"Hang on, before we go any further, I need to make sure I have enough for the deposit." Lee spoke with concern.

Angus set his mind at ease. "The deposit is two hundred dollars and two weeks rent up front."

"I can actually manage that and still eat until I get paid." Lee smiled up at me and I noted that some of the sadness had cleared from his eyes.

"Let's get this done and you can be in by tonight." Angus led Lee down a hallway to his office and I tagged along behind watching the rise and fall of Lee's ass in his tight fitting jeans.

What the fuck was wrong with me, wanting a boy. And yes, he was still a boy, who was way too many years my junior? I felt the familiar sting of jealousy when Angus clutched Lee's bicep and led him to a chair by his desk. The young man's face lit up in a grin, a grin I wanted directed only at me.

I dropped into a chair which was out of the way.

"The lease has the same rent and conditions as the other dancers. I prepared it after you called this morning," Angus said to me.

Lee spun in his seat, a frown on his face. "Am I missing something, Jake?"

Angus sat back in his chair and folded his arms over his chest. He smirked my way and I could almost here him saying "*not again.*" "You haven't told him, have you? Just like you didn't tell the others."

Lee glanced back and forth between us. "Told me what?"

"Will you tell him, or will I?" Angus asked.

I let out a deep breath. I'd hated telling the other men but confessing to Lee terrified me. I was scared to death he'd bolt.

"Roan and I own the building along with the one next to it. We bought them about a year ago and I moved all the dancers in to *Harborside*. The rest of the men said they were happy where they were and didn't want to move."

"You and Roan own the entire block? Two entire blocks of apartments?"

"Yeah, we do."

"That's why the rent is so cheap." Lee turned back to Angus. "The other dancers have the exact same conditions?"

"Exactly the same."

"Okay, where do I sign."

My rapid heartbeat returned to normal and I sagged with relief at Lee's words. I sat quietly while the paperwork was dealt with. When Angus reached the question about next of kin, Lee froze and I stepped up to save him any embarrassment.

"Put me down, Angus. He'll be spending most of his time with the men and me. I can always contact his family if it's anything serious."

My friend raised an eyebrow and gave me a questioning glance. No doubt, I would be interrogated about it later. We had plans for a quiet dinner at his place tonight.

The rest of the signing passed quickly and without incident. Lee handed over his debit card and Angus left us alone while he headed to reception to ask Sarah to process the payment.

"I can't believe I have a decent place to call my own. Thanks for everything, Jake. How do you know Angus?"

"Roan, Angus and I have been good friends since college."

"Is he single?"

"Um....."

Lee cocked his head to one side, he had a puzzled expression on his face. "Surely you know if he's seeing someone."

"Um....." Why wouldn't the fucking words come?

"Oh, fuck! It's you! You two are lovers. Sorry, I didn't mean to move in on you."

Lee stood and was pacing the floor. I grabbed his hand and spun him toward me.

Despite fireworks exploding inside me, I managed to speak.

"You haven't moved in on me, you haven't said or done anything wrong. Relax."

Lee placed a hand on my chest and nodded. The heat from his touch could have burned clear through my damn shirt. I needed to get my head back on fucking straight.

Angus stepped back into the office and I jumped back. It was obvious he'd seen how close we'd been standing and the way my hand rested on Lee's arm while his hand rested against my chest. I sent him what I hoped was a *don't go there*, glare.

"Okay. Keys, contract, card. The place is all yours. Anything you need, contact the office."

Lee accepted everything from Angus, tucked the card and keys away in his pocket and folded the contract before shaking hands and thanking the man.

"I'll see you tonight." I placed a hand on Lee's lower back as I guided him back out to the street. I knew Angus would have more than a few questions for me tonight. Questions I didn't have answers to.

# Chapter Eleven

**LIAM**

"Lunch?" Jake asked.

We were making our way back toward the club alongside each other. There weren't many people out on the streets at this time of day.

"Yeah, that would be nice. My treat as a thank you for the apartment."

"No, save your money. Maybe once you have a steady income we'll have dinner and you can pay."

"Done."

"What would you like?"

"Something light. I'm meeting up with Tommy at 2pm and we'll be working out in the gym later. We were going to use the club gym but I think I'll grab my stuff from the motel, drop it into the apartment and we can use the gym there. Since Tommy lives there too and he's off today, it makes sense."

"Guess so." Jake's voice was deathly quiet.

"What's wrong, Jake?"

He turned to me and cocked an eyebrow. "Nothing, why?"

"You went awfully quiet. Is there something I should know about, Tommy?"

"No, of course not. He's a good guy but he's not into relationships so be careful."

"Neither am I. I'll be fine."

Jake stopped at a small café in a building not far from the club. The sign over the door announced it was the best French café in the city. We stepped inside and made our way to an empty table by the window. I sat down opposite Jake and a waitress appeared seemingly out of thin air. She placed a jug of water and two glasses on the table before handing us both a menu.

"I'll be back shortly." The young woman spoke with a thick French accent.

"Merci, nous serons prêts à commander dans quelques minutes."

Jake spoke in French, none of which I understood except merci, which I knew meant thank you.

"What did you say?"

"I thanked her and told her we'd be ready to order in a few minutes."

I took a cursory glance at the menu. I knew exactly what I would have so I took the opportunity to study Jake instead. Fuck the man was gorgeous. I wished he wasn't out of my league but even if he hadn't been, no-one would want to be with a man like me. Sadness at the thought of being alone, never having anyone special in my life, washed over me. If only I could turn back the clock.

I was still deep in thought when the waitress returned and asked what we would like. I ordered a ham and cheese croissant with a bowl of potato and leek soup. Jake ordered the same and we both asked for sparkling mineral water to wash it all down. I wasn't much of a coffee lover but did adore a hot chocolate with marshmallows floating on the top every now and again.

After the waitress left the table, Jake sat back and folded his arms across his chest. He sat for a moment, studying me. The same way I'd studied him. I began to feel uncomfortable under his gaze.

"So, you and Angus, huh?"

"You could say that."

Okay, now I was confused. "What do you mean?"

Jake took a large gulp of his water before piercing me with his eyes and thinking for a moment. "Hmm, why do you expect me to answer your questions but you won't answer any of mine?"

Nope. I was not going to be cornered into telling him something I didn't want him to know.

"Fair enough, I was just making conversation."

Jake tilted his head to the side and I was forced to drop my eyes to my lap to avoid his stare. I heard him sigh before he spoke.

"Angus and I are good friends who spend time together when we need to. No strings. Mutual benefit. Neither of us is interested in a long-term relationship. What we have works for us."

I nodded my understanding as bowls of steaming hot soup were placed in front of us. I dipped the spoon into the thick broth and tentatively sipped at it, mindful of burning my mouth. Problem was, it smelled so damn good and I was eager to taste it. I thanked the young woman when she placed the croissants and mineral water on the table.

"Will that be all?" she asked.

"Yes, thank you." Jake answered for both of us.

I decided to attack the warm pastry while waiting for the soup to cool.

"Did you work last night?" I asked Jake.

"Nope. Roan worked it and he has today and tomorrow. I do Wednesday and Thursday. Roan has Friday and Saturday then, we alternate the following week. After five years, it's starting to wear on us though. I'm going to talk with him about hiring someone on, it's not like we can't afford it."

I swallowed the bite of croissant I'd just taken. "It must be exhausting."

"It is and it seems like we spend our days off catching up on sleep."

"Is Roan gay?"

"Yes, he is. Mom says she struck the jackpot having two sons who are gay because we're both happy to go shopping with her and help her pick out clothes and furnishings. She insists we have better taste than most females she knows."

"What about your dad?"

"He's great." Jake laughed. "He loves the fact we save him the torture of shopping with Mom."

I joined in his laughing. "It sounds like you have a great family." I know I sounded wistful and Jake was quick to snatch the opportunity.

"Lee, did you're family kick you out because you're gay?"

I snapped my head up and locked eyes with him. "What? No! They don't even know I'm gay."

"Is that why you don't see them? Are you afraid of what they'd say?"

"No. Two of my uncles are gay and they're Mom and Dad's best friends. Please, Jake, don't ask me questions I can't answer."

Jake tilted his head to the side. "Can't or won't?"

"Both. Please, let it go."

"Very well, I'll do as you ask."

"Thank you."

"Subject change. What do you like to do in your spare time?"

I pushed the empty plate away and pulled the now warm soup back in front of me. I moaned as the broth slid down my throat. It was smooth, creamy with a bite from the pepper which had been added. It was almost as good as Dad made. Almost.

"Spare time? Doesn't seem like I'll have much. Between learning to dance, the gym and doing the books, I reckon the only thing I'll be interested in will be sleep."

"If you do find time, what will you do?"

"I'll probably get in some swimming, I love the water. The barbecue area at the complex will be an ideal spot to sit and read or do a few crosswords. What about you?"

"I visit Mom and Dad on at least one of my days off. Mom and I usually go shopping, have lunch out and have a manicure. Back at their place we have dinner and I watch some television and catch up on gossip with dad before I leave. Roan visits at least once a week too and it's pretty much the same for him. On birthdays, Thanksgiving, Christmas and at Easter, we make a point of all being together. If one of us should be at the club, we ask Joey to look after things for us. Apart from that, I love to swim and I work out in the gym."

"What about when you're with Angus?"

"We have dinner together. Sometimes we'll go dancing or watch a movie and we spend the night together at either my place or his."

"Where do you live?"

Jake didn't answer and I realized, I'd crossed a line. After all, he was my boss.

"Sorry, shouldn't have asked."

"No, it's okay. I live in one of the penthouses in the apartment block next to *Harborside*. Roan has the other. Angus lives downstairs. It's a similar building to yours only there are four floors. It's called, Harbor Gardens."

We finished our soup and Jake glanced at his watch.

"I need to get going so Roan can make his meeting. Are you headed back to the club?"

"No. I'm going back to the motel. I'll let them know I'm leaving, might even get some money back. I'll drop my stuff in at the apartment and then meet up with Tommy."

"I'll get the check and walk back with you."

Jake paid for our meal and we made our way back to the club and motel. After thanking Jake for the meal and his help with the apartment, I crossed the road and headed for reception to speak with the motel manager. I could almost feel Jake's eyes burning into my back as I walked away.

*** 

I explained about the apartment to the motel manager and he agreed to refund me three of the next four nights I had booked. I'd thanked him profusely and assured him, if I was in need of a motel again, I wouldn't hesitate to be in touch. I grabbed my belongings, locked the door and hurried down the road to my new home.

Excitement gripped me as I jogged up the stairs, unlocked the door and stepped inside. I couldn't believe it was truly mine. Well, mine, Jake's and the agents. I dropped the duffle on the floor, crossed the living room, unlocked and opened one of the glass sliding doors. There were two Adirondack chairs with a small table between them. I could picture myself with a beer, relaxing and enjoying the view. I pulled my phone from the pocket of my jeans before I planted my ass in one of the chairs. I pulled up Tommy's number and sent him a quick text to see if he wanted to meet me in the small coffee shop downstairs instead of uptown. His answer came back seconds later. He was in his apartment and said he was ready to meet up at any time. I asked him to give me twenty minutes to unpack and I'd be there.

I dragged myself out of the chair, grabbed the duffle bag and padded through to the bedroom. I decided to use the first one I came to. It took all of ten minutes to unpack my meager belongings. Once done, I stashed the bag on the top shelf of the closet and returned to sit on the bed, contemplating my change of fortune for a few minutes.

I would make this work. I would make myself into a man my parents could finally be proud of and hopefully, one day, I might even go home to see them. Tears pricked my eyes. I missed my family and wondered how they were.

Did Steve and Keegan have a child on the way? Was I to be an uncle? Were any of them missing me? Would Steve look for me again? If he finds me, what will I do? So many questions.

Bringing my pity party to an end, I swiped away the tears which had fallen, headed into the bathroom and splashed cold water on my face. Feeling marginally better, I headed downstairs to meet Tommy. I was determined not to let Jake down. For some reason, he had faith in me, even though he didn't know me from a bar of soap. I resolved to be the best dancer he'd ever laid eyes on. For the first time in my life, I would make someone proud of me.

*** 

I asked at the counter for Tommy and a young man pointed out where he was seated at a table which had a view over the harbor. He also informed me that Tommy had ordered hot chocolates for both of us. I thanked him and headed to the table.

"Tommy?"

Tommy stood and I had to stop the groan which bubbled in my throat. I'd accepted the fact the club only employed beautiful men but the man who stood before me had all the traits of a super model. He was so far out of the realm of handsome, there was no word for him. He was tall, around six and a half feet. His eyes were rich brown and his long almost black hair was tied back in a ponytail. When he smiled at me, I couldn't believe the depth of his dimples. Fuck, you could have filled them with water and sailed boats in there. His golden skin was perfect, not a blotch marred it. He was dressed in a loose pair of sweats and a hoodie which was a shame, I would have loved to ogle his curves.

He thrust his hand toward me and we shook.

"Lee, nice to meet you. I ordered for us, hope you like chocolate."

"Love it, thank you."

We both took a seat and the young man from the counter slid our mugs of chocolate onto the table. Two marshmallows sat on the saucer to one side. I immediately dropped mine into the hot liquid. Tommy ate his like candy and took a gulp of his drink before speaking.

"Okay. You've decided you'd like me to work with you. Like a personal trainer. Is that right?"

"Yes, at least for a while. I've managed to work out on and off but mainly things like rowing, jogging, cycling. More fitness than strength building and not with any supervision or advice. I'd be happy to pay you."

"No, consider it my pleasure. I'll enjoy watching your ass in a pair of tight shorts."

I felt my face heat and Tommy laughed.

"You're ready to start today?"

"Yep, I'll need to change first. I don't have shorts but I have sweats."

"They'll do fine. I'll use my imagination to fill in the gaps."

My face heated again and Tommy closed his hand over mine. It didn't have the same effect as when Jake touched me, although it wasn't unpleasant.

"You're gonna have to lose your modesty if you want to make a living as a stripper, Honey. Guess we'll work on that too while we're together."

I nodded, too embarrassed for words.

"I'm happy to instruct you but I have a couple of rules I won't allow you to break."

"They are?"

"First – you do exactly as I say. When I tell you enough, you stop what you're doing. Second – you train three times a week only and you have a full days' break between training sessions. With the dancing, you don't need to work strength any more often. You can run or do aerobic exercise on the other days if you like."

"You seem to know a lot about this."

"My dad owned a gym before he died, I spent every waking moment in the place."

"I'm sorry."

"It was a long time ago now, but thanks. Finish your drink and we'll get started."

I drank the rest of the thick creamy chocolate. It was delicious. I was gonna have to stay away from this place or I could envision myself gaining so much weight, they'd have to reinforce the stage.

# Chapter Twelve

**LIAM**

I had no idea how long Tommy had been working me. The burn in my arm muscles was downright painful and my legs were shaking from the effort of holding me up. I didn't know how I was still standing. Sweat poured off me and I longed for a swim in the neighboring pool.

"You're done." Tommy threw a towel in my direction and I wiped my face dry.

I plopped down on the floor and sucked in large gulps of air to placate my protesting lungs. "Fuck, this is gonna either make me stronger or kill me."

"Wait until tomorrow. If history repeats itself, you'll barely be able to walk. I know the others could hardly put one foot in front of the other for the first couple of weeks. There are showers in the back of the gym. I have a couple of pair of swim shorts in a locker back there so I'll loan you some. The water in the pool will be cold and will help prevent some of the soreness. I suggest you take a cold shower when you wake in the morning too."

Tommy held out his hand and pulled me to my feet. My breathing was still labored while he wasn't puffed enough to blow out a candle and he'd done everything with me. My legs shook as we headed toward the showers and when I stumbled, Tommy managed to grab me before my face became one with the floor. He held me against his chest and I gazed into his eyes for a moment. They burned with lust and it terrified me.

"Sorry." I pushed back and hurried away.

Tommy caught up with me and took me by the arm, forcing me to face him.

"Lee, are you okay?"

"I'm fine."

He studied me for a moment before stepping over to a bank of lockers and opening one. He pulled out a pair of brightly colored, very small shorts and handed them to me. I held them up and burst into laughter.

"Are you kidding me?"

"They stretch." Tommy reached back into the locker and pulled out a similar pair for himself.

I shrugged and stepped into a shower stall. The hot water felt good on my aching muscles. I knew cold would be better but the warmth seeped deep into my bones and relaxed the tension. A dispenser containing body wash, shampoo and conditioner was fixed to the wall and I squirted a generous amount of wash into my hands.

I was deep in thought about Tommy when a loud bang at the door caused me to jump.

"Come on, Princess. You don't need that long in there."

I hurriedly turned off the water and stepped into the dry area off to one side of the small area. After drying myself off, I wrestled to get the tiny shorts onto my slightly damp body. Once in place, I wasn't sure I could wear them in public. Even though, at this time of the afternoon, no-one was around. They were tight and hugged my package, leaving nothing to the imagination. The back slid into the crack, leaving half my ass on display. I made a mental note to hit the store for a pair which were slightly more modest. I gathered up the towel, my folded gym clothes and shoes and stepped out to where Tommy was waiting. My eyes traveled over his body, appreciating how well-defined every muscle was. His shorts clung to him like a second skin. Goddamn, he was easy on the eyes.

He was smirking when I raised my gaze back to his face and I felt my cheeks heat with embarrassment. Tommy reached out and gathered my hand. I didn't pull away. In fact, I rather liked him touching me.

"You're warm. I said cold showers for a couple of days."

I dropped my head, feeling guilty.

"I hate cold showers."

"It doesn't matter, you need to look after your muscles. Heat will feel good initially but won't help with any strains or swelling. Do I need to shower with you to make sure you do as I ask?"

I snapped my eyes to his and saw the mischief dancing in them. I wondered if I could maybe develop something with this man. Nothing too serious. Something like Jake shared with Angus. The thought of my sexy boss caused my stomach to clench but I shook off the crazy feelings. Nothing. Absolutely nothing was happening there. I would be a fool to even contemplate it.

*** 

I dived into the pool and speared back to the surface with a gasp. The water was fucking freezing despite the warmth of the day. Tommy's head broke the surface close to me a moment later.

"Fucking hell! Is the fucking heating broken?"

Tommy laughed.

"This pool is only heated during the winter months. Stop complaining, the cold is refreshing."

"Refreshing, my ass."

My dick was trying to climb up inside me and my balls had shrivelled to the size of marbles. Tommy bounced closer to me and wrapped a hand around my waist. I shivered, not knowing if it was because of the ice cold of the water or his touch. We locked eyes. The mischief of earlier was gone, replaced with smoldering lust.

"Tommy," I whispered.

"Go with it, Baby."

He lowered his head and his lips sought out mine. It felt different, I'd only ever kissed women before. He kept his eyes on me, watching cautiously. When I didn't pull away, or fight him off, he moved closer. Placing a hand to each side of my face, he tilted my head and his kiss became more insistent. I rested my hands on his biceps. When his tongue skimmed along the seam, I parted my lips slightly. His tongue slithered inside to find mine and I finally reacted and joined in.

I guessed, kissing was kissing whether it was with a man or a woman. Wrapping my arms around his waist, I held him closer. Our tongues commenced a slow dance, exploring each other's mouths. My hands moved from his waist to tangle in his wet locks. When I tugged on the strands, Tommy moaned.

We could have continued for hours but a discreet cough had us jumping apart as if we'd been burned.

I looked up to see Jenkins, one of the bar staff and another man I hadn't met before.

"Don't mind us," Jenkins laughed.

Tommy flipped him the bird as both men jumped in and swam over to us.

"Lee, this is Neil. He's a waiter at the club." Jenkins turned to Neil. "This is the new dancer I told you about with the smokin' hot body."

Neil nodded. "Pleased to meet you. Do you have an apartment in the complex or are you here with Tommy?"

"Yeah, just moved in a couple of hours ago. Jake organized it for me."

"He did the same for us. He's a good boss and a good man," Jenkins said.

"I can't believe I can afford it. After the last place I lived in, it's like fucking paradise."

The other men laughed and Tommy said, "I know what you mean."

"We'll let you two get back to whatever you were doing. We're here to swim a few before we work tonight."

"Same," Tommy and I said in unison before I said bye and swam off.

***

Tommy and I headed upstairs side by side.

"What are your plans for dinner?" Tommy asked.

"I don't have any but I do know it will be an early night. I'm back at work tomorrow."

"How about we order in pizza and watch a movie."

"Pizza?"

"Yeah, I indulge now and again. Mostly, I maintain a strict diet so I can afford to spoil myself occasionally."

"Sounds good to me. Your place or mine?"

"Mine?"

"Okay. Give me time to take a shower and dress and I'll be down in a few. What number are you?"

"217. Turn left from the elevators and I'm four doors down the corridor on the left."

We reached the landing to the second floor and I stopped.

"I'll be down in twenty?"

"Sounds good. I'll order, what do you like?"

"Pepperoni."

"My favorite."

I turned to start up the last flight of steps when Tommy called out.

"Cold, Lee, or I'll have to supervise."

"Whatever," I mumbled.

I could still hear his laughter halfway upstairs. The man was a fucking sadist. Yeah, I knew what he was telling me was right, but did I mention how much I hated cold water on my body?

I unlocked the door and flung it open. I still couldn't believe I was living here. Hopefully, everything would work out with the dancing because there was no way I could afford this on a bookkeeper's salary.

***

Tommy's door was ajar when I arrived at his apartment. I called out before stepping inside.

"Tommy?"

"Bedroom. Won't be a minute. Have a seat."

I parked my ass on one of the leather sofas and took in the surroundings. The apartment was

158

identical to mine but reversed. Where my sofa was positioned to the right as you entered, Tommy's was to the left. His views were over the city but I could see glimpses of the harbor through the dining area window.

He appeared from the hallway wearing sweats and a polo shirt and looking good enough to eat. I shimmied over slightly when he chose to sit down beside me. Tucking one leg underneath himself, he swivelled to face me. I noted a small notebook in his hand.

"What's that?"

"This is a list of your workout so, when I'm not around you can still get it done. Remember, take a full day's break between, warm up and down to prevent injury and cold shower or swim."

He handed me the book and I flipped open to the first page. He'd listed what he'd taught me today.

1. 20 body weight squats.
2. 10 push ups.
3. 20 walking lunges.
4. 10 dumbbell rows (using 10-20-pound weight.)
5. 15 second plank.
6. 30 jumping Jacks.
7. Repeat for 3 rounds.

I stuffed it back in my pocket.

"Fuck."

"What's wrong?"

"I was meant to go with Jake and get new books for work today. I totally forgot. I'll leave earlier in the morning and pick them up on the way to the office."

"I'm sure Jake will understand. You were probably distracted with the apartment and all."

I nodded but couldn't help feeling I'd let Jake down. Silly, I know.

"Tell me about yourself, Lee. Where are you from? How did you end up here? I want to hear it all."

I felt myself stiffen at his curiosity but knew I was bound to be asked questions for a few weeks while my new colleagues got to know me.

"Linton. I was working part-time in a Chinese Restaurant and studying Accounting in college. It didn't work out. I thought it would be easier to get work here in the city. I arrived on Friday night and was staying in the motel across the road from the club. I was woken by an argument between Jake and a customer."

"Rick."

"Yeah. I get the feeling it wasn't a onetime only thing."

"Nope. It happens every time he and his wife argue. He's harmless really."

"That's when I met Jake. He asked me if I was interested in dancing and I laughed. I've done a bit of gymnastics but never danced. He insisted I could be taught. I thought – why not? Pedro and Chris are teaching me some Devil and Angel routines but it's been slow going. I struggle to support my weight for the tricks."

"That's why you asked about strength training?"

"Yeah. The moves aren't a huge issue because I can do the splits and I'm pretty flexible. It's just trying not to fall on my face because my arms give way."

"This workout will help with that. If you like swimming, that will strengthen your arms too."

"I love swimming when the water isn't cold enough to turn my fucking dick to a popsicle."

Tommy laughed.

"How old are you?"

"I'll be eighteen in five months' time. November 22nd. That's why Jake is keeping me in the office during opening times. He said dancing when I'm eighteen is risky enough but the cops will accept it as long as I don't work the floor where there's alcohol and gambling. Until then, I'll keep the books. Both Roan and Jake hate doing them and to be honest, they're pretty bad at it too. I need new books because the ones they have are a mess."

"I've heard them complaining about them on more than one occasion. You'll have to be careful they don't tie you to a chair and keep you in the office."

I laughed and at the same time, a buzzer sounded from a panel fitted on the wall by the front door. Tommy stood, crossed the floor, pressed a button and spoke into the contraption.

"Come on up."

I heard another buzzing sound and Tommy turned to say, "Did Jake show you how to work the security?"

"No, I'll figure it out. Mom and Dad's home had one. It's not rocket science."

Moments later a boy appeared at the now opened front door. Tommy paid him, obviously giving him a decent tip if the smile on his face was anything to go by. He accepted the brown cardboard box, thanked the kid and closed the door.

"Need a plate?" Tommy held the box in the air.

"No. Have you got napkins?"

"Yep, I'll grab some."

Tommy placed the box on the coffee table and headed for the kitchen. He returned with a bundle of white paper napkins and handed a couple to me. He also placed a couple of sodas on the small table. He threw back the lid of the box and we both helped ourselves to a piece. I took a huge bite, surprised to find, I was actually really hungry.

"Do your parents live in Linton?"

I hesitated, I hadn't meant to mention my family.

"No, Paxton. We don't speak."

Tommy seemed to understand, there would be no further discussion about them.

"Tell me about you. How did you come to be a dancer?"

Tommy took a bite of pizza before setting it on a napkin on the table. "I started dancing when I was thirteen."

"Thirteen?"

"My parents were addicts and they 'sold' me to their dealer, Draco. They couldn't afford to pay him for the drugs they'd already used. He had a strip club in the industrial area over the other side of town. It was all hush hush because he dealt drugs and guns out of the place. It was more of a free for all brothel than strip club and his clientele liked young boys. I lost my innocence less than four hours after I arrived."

"Oh, fuck, Tommy. I'm so sorry."

"I fought Draco on everything and eventually he stuck me with drugs so I obeyed him. I was in a daze most of the time, too weak to fight him any longer. I was there for five years. He had one of the older boys teach me to dance, not on a pole though. It was more of a strip routine until we were naked. I was fucked at least three times a night. During the day, Draco used me as his personal whore."

Hot tears rolled over my cheeks. What had happened to Tommy suddenly put my life into perspective. I began to realize how fortunate I'd been. Had my behaviour been no better than that of a spoiled rotten prick?

"How did you get away?"

"The cops raided the place. There was a shootout. Draco was killed along with most of his goons. In the commotion, I managed to slip away. I spent the next six months on the streets, picking up a bit of work here and there. The first few weeks were a nightmare as I went through withdrawal from whatever drugs Draco had me on. I met Roan when he caught me stealing from a local store. He paid for the candy bars, took me outside and said I was going with him. Jake and he were in the process of setting up the club for opening and he took me back there. Thank God." He took a deep, shuddering breath.

"Weren't you worried it was like the place you'd just escaped from?"

"Not really. There was something about Roan and his brother that made me trust them. They got me cleaned up and took me to see a doctor to have a bunch of tests run. He said I was underweight and malnourished but I'd recover in no time. Roan took me back to his place and took care of me until I was strong enough to take care of myself. He also taught me to dance using the pole and had me working out in the gym. He's a trained counsellor so, we talked everything out during weekly sessions until he was satisfied I'd put the past to rest. Being able to discuss what had happened with him made a huge difference because I hated myself for what I'd done. Jake offered me a permanent job, set me up here and the rest is pretty much history."

"What happened to your parents?"

"Draco had one of his men kill them just after we left."

"I'm so sorry, Tommy."

"Don't be. The day I met Roan was the day I finally started living. I love those brothers more than anything on Earth and I can never repay them for saving me."

We ate in silence for the next few minutes. Was Jake right? Could I get over my past by confiding in one of the brothers? It would have to be Roan if I did. I wouldn't be able to bear the look of disgust in Jake's eyes.

# Chapter Thirteen

**JAKE**

I found Roan at the bar chatting with Trace when I returned from having lunch with Lee and wandered over to join the men who were deep in conversation.

"Jake, all set with your new boy?"

I straddled a stool and Trace set a bottle of water in front of me.

"Yep, all signed up. He's meeting with Tommy shortly to sort out what he can do in the gym to build his strength. He has the appearance of a man but isn't yet fully developed."

"He'll be fucking sensational when his body matures. I mean, the kid is a killer already. Wait until you see him, Roan. He'll have you drooling within seconds of meeting him."

"Knock it off, Trace. Nobody will be drooling over him," I growled.

Trace and my brother both snapped their eyes toward me, a questioning expression on their faces. Roan's eyes did that searching thing they did when he suspected I wasn't telling him the full story about something.

"Something we should know?" Roan asked.

"No," I snapped.

"You sure?" he persisted.

"He's a kid, Roan. Barely legal."

"It doesn't mean you can't nurture an interest until he's eighteen. I mean, it's only a few months away."

"Roan," I warned.

"I'm gonna have to meet this kid who has you acting so defensive. I might have to ask him a few questions since my brother won't say anything. When's he in?"

"Tomorrow and you won't be asking any questions. Leave him alone. Mind your own business. Don't you have a meeting to get to?"

"Canceled."

"Go home then, I'll stay."

I spun on my heels and stomped to my office before Roan could pepper me with any more questions. He could read me like a book and would already sense that I felt an attraction to Lee. An attraction which couldn't be acted on.

I dragged my fingers over my scalp and dropped into the chair behind my desk. It was gonna be a long fucking afternoon. I was due to meet Angus for dinner after the eight o'clock show. Maybe I'd get Trace and Joey to look after things and lock up. A night in bed with my friend was sure to put out the fire in my body. A fire which had been on a slow smolder since Lee had first crossed the road and headed toward me.

The door opened and Roan poked his head through.

"Can I come in?"

"Sure."

He stepped in, closed the door and dropped into the chair opposite.

"Are you okay?"

"Of course, I am. Why do you ask?"

"You seem bothered. Is it Lee?"

I sighed, sat back in the chair and folded my arms over my chest.

"It's strange. My body reacts whenever he's around and I don't understand why. I mean, I'm happy with what Angus and I have."

"Are you?"

"Yes. I'm not interested in a serious relationship. Angus and I get along well, we love each other and fulfil each other's needs."

"Hmm, maybe."

"What do you mean, maybe?"

"Maybe Lee is your future. It might be why you've felt attracted to him since you met. Fate. Soul mates. We all have one, we just have to find them."

"Don't be ridiculous. That's stuff for books and movies, not real life."

"Scoff all you like little brother but you'll see soon enough. You have a look in your eyes when Lee's name is mentioned that I've never seen before."

"Whatever. How are you and Ken working out?"

Roan shrugged. "Let's just say, he's not my soul mate. I'll have to keep searching."

"I don't understand. You said you were great together and you were gonna ask him to move in. What happened?"

"Phil happened."

"Who the fuck is Phil?"

"Ken's bit on the side."

"Oh, I'm sorry."

Roan stood and smiled down at me. "Don't be. It's all good. I met Jace at the gym last night. He's new to town and we're having dinner tonight."

I shook my head and laughed. "I can't keep up with you. That reminds me, I'm leaving the club with Trace and Joey after the eight o'clock show. Angus and I are having dinner and spending the night together."

"I don't know why when you know I'm right. Lee's the man for you. You'll see."

"Were you leaving?"

"Anxious to get rid of me because you can't face the truth."

I scowled and Roan made a hasty escape through the door.

Once I was alone, I wondered if there was any truth to his words before laughing it off. Lee and I would never have anything serious between us. The man was far too young for me and there was something in his past which would prevent him from ever having a future with anyone if he didn't talk with someone about it.

***

Sam had the eight o'clock show, Dixon, the eight thirty. I sat on a stool at the bar watching Dixon and the goings on in the club. Balati slid onto the stool next to me. Monday nights were our quietest and it gave me an opportunity to catch up with the staff.

I spun to face the huge man. I swear to God; his arms were the size of tree trunks. I didn't usually turn away if someone tried to intimidate me but he was one man I wouldn't have hesitated to run from. I'd seen him haul men into the air using only one hand. Men who were over six feet tall and weighed around two hundred and fifty pounds. Put it this way, I was really, *really* glad he worked with me and not against me.

"How's it goin', Boss?"

"Good. Like usual, I'm looking forward to some time off."

"I don't know why you don't hire someone else. Me and the rest of the boys would make sure they did the right thing by ya."

"I intend to discuss it with Roan in the next day or so. We can't keep this pace up for much longer."

The customers began clapping and whistling wildly. I realized Dixon was finished and I could head out to meet up with Angus. He was cooking dinner for us at his place because he insisted, he didn't want to get dressed up to go out. I hadn't argued, I could do with the quiet night in.

I stood up from the stool. "I'm leaving early tonight. Trace and Joey are closing, can you make sure they're okay?"

"Sure, Boss. Have a good evening."

I slapped the man on the shoulder and thanked him. As I passed Trace who was serving a customer, I tapped my hand on the bar.

"Call me if there are any problems."

"We'll be fine. Have a nice evening, Boss."

I left the club and headed into the night. The air was warm, tinged with salt from the nearby water. I loved everything about this city. I was happy here and had everything I could want - a loving family, a prosperous club and the best staff of men one could ask for. Yep, I had everything I wanted. Or, did I?

I shook the ridiculous question from my mind and headed to where Angus would be waiting. As I strode past *Harborside*, I couldn't help but wonder about what Lee might be doing. Was he alone? Why did I care? Fuck, I'd asked myself so many questions since I'd met Lee, I felt like a quiz show was taking place inside my head.

I reached the gate to Harbor Gardens, punched in the code and it swung open. Once inside, I hurried to the heavy wooden entrance door which had an ornate brass handle. I punched in another code and pushed the door open. I ignored the elevators like usual and took the stairs two at a time until I reached the third floor.

The door to Angus's apartment was unlocked and I let myself in.

I was assaulted with a myriad of spicy scents and knew Angus was making my favorite – Indian Butter Chicken, Basmati Rice with Naan bread and there would be a good red wine. I found Angus in the kitchen stirring a pot on the stove top. He was wearing a pair of tight black boxer briefs and an apron. I kicked off my shoes, stripped off my socks and shirt and padded over to him.

He turned as I approached and I kissed him gently.

"Smells delicious, Sweetheart."

Angus looked me up and down.

"Overdressed, don't you think?"

I laughed, headed back to the living room and undressed down to my dark purple boxer briefs.

"Better," Angus laughed.

"I'll just wash up."

"Okay, I'll be dishing up so don't be long."

"Mere moments."

I hurried to a small powder room where I washed my hands and face. I then returned to the dining room where Angus was standing, opening a bottle of wine. Our food was in large dishes, steam curled above them.

While Angus finished pouring the wine, I sat. My mouth watered as the mingling scents tortured my nostrils. As soon as he was seated, we both unfolded napkins onto our laps. While Angus sipped at the wine, I dug into the food. It didn't disappoint. The chicken, like always was so tender it melted in my mouth. The spices had been added in the perfect combination to tantalize the taste buds. I groaned as the first mouthful made its way down my throat.

Angus laughed.

"Anyone hearing you groan would think you were getting a blow job."

"They can think whatever they like. Fuck I love this meal." I forked up another huge mouthful and groaned with delight as the spices again danced on my tongue.

We ate in silence for a few moments and then Angus hit me with both barrels, like I'd known he would.

"What's going on with, Lee? Don't tell me nothing, I saw how you were in the office."

I sipped at the wine. "Honestly, there's nothing. I've known him since Saturday morning and haven't seen him for more than a few hours since he left on Saturday night. When you left the office to take his payment, he asked a few questions about you. He seemed to think there was something serious between us. I needed to stop him from pacing and mumbling about moving in on my territory. I was holding him against me so I could set him straight. I explained we were good friends with benefits." I didn't miss the disappointment in Angus's eyes and wondered what it meant.

"Yeah, that's what we are."

Angus appeared to have fallen into a funk.

"What's wrong, Sweetheart?"

"Nothing. So, do you think there could be something between you two?"

I placed the glass I'd been sipping from back onto the table.

"Did you see him? Did you take note of his age? I'm a twenty-six-year-old man, he's a seventeen-year-old boy."

"So?"

"It's too big an age gap and even if I was a couple of years younger, he's a virgin. I'm not even sure he's accepted the fact he's gay."

"We were both virgins the first time we fucked."

"Yeah, we *both* were. And, only a few months separated our ages. How I might feel makes no difference anyway."

"Why not?"

"He's spending time with Tommy."

"Ah, Casanova."

"Exactly. Maybe he'd be better off with Tommy, he's only twenty-three. They'd be good together."

"You keep telling yourself that, Babe. You might even convince yourself it's true. No, the little I saw today showed me, there's a connection between you two. I think he's a good fit for you, despite the difference in age."

I finished my meal and folded the napkin, resting it alongside the plate. "Don't you fucking start with fate and soul mate shit. I had enough of that from Roan earlier."

Angus shrugged before standing. "Help me clear this away and I'll help you forget about Lee and anyone else who might be on your mind. Are you staying the night?"

"Would you mind?"

"I'd never mind you staying here. Let's get this cleaned up so I can take you to bed and show you just how much I don't mind."

Angus leaned forward and brushed his lips over mine. I carried the dishes in my hands to the sink and began rinsing them off so they could be stacked in the dishwasher.

# Chapter Fourteen

**LIAM**

"Lee, Baby, wake up."

I felt someone shaking me. I was snuggled against something hard but soft at the same time. I moved to cuddle in closer and heard a man laugh.

"Baby, as much as I'm enjoying this, it's time for you to go to home."

"I don't want to go to home," I grumbled.

A strong pair of hands pushed me into a sitting position. I pushed through the fog of my brain and opened my eyes. Glancing around, I finally realized where I was. The television I'd been watching was switched off and only the soft glow of a lamp lit the room. I sat back into the sofa, scrubbing my hands down my face.

"Sorry. How long was I asleep?"

"Don't be. I rather enjoyed having you in my arms, Babe. You crashed into sleep about ten minutes after the movie started so, a couple of hours. You're probably exhausted after doing unfamiliar exercise."

"I guess so." I pushed to my feet but my legs felt like noodles. I stumbled and crashed down onto Tommy's lap. His arms wrapped around me.

"If you want to stay, Baby, you're welcome to."

"I'm so fucking tired." I dropped my forehead to Tommy's chest.

He placed two fingers under my chin and gazed into my eyes. "You can stay in the guest room if you like."

I nodded, not sure I'd manage to get upstairs to my own apartment without falling and breaking my damn neck. I was so bloody exhausted.

Tommy brushed his lips over mine and pushed me onto my feet. His hands remained on my waist, holding me steady. With an arm around my waist, he led me through to his guest room. I plonked myself on the bed and sat staring at the wall opposite. I didn't even have the energy to get myself into the bathroom to brush my teeth.

"Come on. I have a spare toothbrush in the bathroom and you'll thank me when you wake up in the morning without pizza pasted to your teeth." Ignoring my protests, he pulled me back onto my feet.

In the bathroom, Tommy handed me a toothbrush and paste. I rested my hands on the sink, supporting myself

"Will you be okay?"

Tommy stood watching me in the mirror. Raising one hand, I waved over my shoulder. "I'll be fine. Thanks."

He left the bathroom and I stared down at the brush and paste, trying to remember what I was supposed to do with them.

I slid to the floor, closed my eyes and was out like a light.

***

I stirred awake wrapped around a warm body and wondered where the hell I was and what had I done? My arm was draped across a hard chest, one leg thrown across a bulging thigh, our morning wood nestled into each other, separated only by the briefs we were wearing. I searched my memory for where I'd been the previous night.

"Tommy," I murmured.

"Hmm."

I peeled my eyes open and lifted my head, our sleep fogged eyes met.

"Fuck."

"Hmm, no we didn't actually."

I breathed a sigh of relief. It wasn't that I'd mind being fucked, or fucking Tommy, and I suspected it would happen, but I didn't want to be semi-comatose when it did. I pushed myself up into a sitting position and rested my head on the wall at the back of the bed.

"How did I get here?"

"You passed out in the bathroom and my bedroom was closest. You aren't exactly a lightweight."

"Sorry, guess I was more exhausted than I realized."

I stared down at Tommy. His long dark hair fanned out in tangles over the white pillow, a few strands hung over his eyes. Reaching down, I pushed them back. The sheet lay across his hips and I grabbed the opportunity to take a close look at the man. His skin molded to the ridges and peaks of hard muscle. His waist and hips were narrow and the gutters to each side of his belly, enticed one to follow where they led. The sheet tented, his dick searching for a way to push free. I licked my lips. Just one look. Did I have the guts to throw back the sheet and take him into my hand?

"Do it."

My eyes snapped to Tommy's.

"What?"

182

"Get rid of the sheet and take me in your hands. Have you ever had a man's dick in your hands?"

My cheeks heated and I shook my head. I'd been down on a few women, sucked at pussy, but I'd never had the courage to follow through with a man.

Tommy flung the sheet back and my eyes zeroed in on his bobbing dick. He lifted one of my hands in his and guided it into place. I wrapped my palm around him. The skin was smooth and as soft as satin. A contrast to his hardness which was more like a steel post. I grazed my thumb over the slit and felt the wetness of a droplet of pre-cum. I raised my eyes to his face. His eyes were clouded with lust and searched my face for any indication I might be feeling uncomfortable.

My hand seemed to develop a mind of its own and slid over the length, back and forth. The hard ridge rubbed against my palm. More droplets of milky fluid erupted from the slit and slid over the head. I used them as lube. I twisted my fingers and tugged at the same time. It caused Tommy to gasp and call out. My hand jerked back, I was sure I must have hurt him.

"Don't stop, Lee. It feels fucking amazing."

I lowered my hand back to his dick which had been waving from one side of his belly to the other, searching me out. Tommy lifted his hips, pushing his cock back and forth. He hardened even further, something I hadn't thought possible. Sweat beaded, causing his body to shimmer in the soft light of the bedroom. When he pushed my hand away, I groaned with disappointment.

"On your back, Lee."

I did as he asked and Tommy rolled over on top of me, supporting himself on his hands to prevent his entire weight from crushing me.

"Look at me."

I peered at his face.

"Tell me if you want to stop at any time and I will. Do you want this?"

"Yes, please, Tommy. Make me a man."

Tommy nodded and reached over to a side table. He opened a drawer and pulled out a condom and bottle of lube which he threw on the bed next to us. When he moved back over my body, he lowered his lips to mine. I opened for him immediately and his tongue plunged inside. I was getting the hang of kissing a man and enjoyed fighting for dominance. Our kiss became frantic. Teeth clashed. Moans filled the silence of the bedroom. Our cocks leaked with excitement and caressed each other as our bodies meshed together. I felt an orgasm building and my balls tucked up tight.

We drew apart, gasping for breath. Tommy sat back on his haunches and I immediately felt the loss.

"Roll over, Baby."

I turned over and he grabbed my hips, pulling my ass into the air. I buried my face in the pillow as his hands caressed my hard, rounded cheeks.

"Fucking beautiful."

I heard the flick of a cap and a moment later, almost catapulted from the bed when a thick finger slid inside me.

"Relax, Baby." Tommy placed a hand on the base of my back, leaned over me and placed a kiss on my cheek. "We can stop any time you like."

"No, keep going."

My hole was stretched wider as the finger twisted and pushed. I lifted my ass to push back against it. When a second finger pushed inside to join the first, it felt fucking amazing. My muscles relaxed as they accepted the intrusion. My cock leaked like a faucet. I could feel the wetness against the muscles of my belly and I danced on the edge of an orgasm.

Tommy leaned close to my ear and whispered, "You feel so good. Almost ready for me."

When a third finger entered me, I squirmed and bucked, wanting more.

"Tommy."

"Yes, Baby."

"More, please. I need more."

"More what, Baby?"

"I don't know. It's just not enough."

I pushed my hand beneath me and wrapped eager fingers around my weeping cock. Tommy pulled it away and pushed both arms over my head. I was beginning to know what torture felt like. His fingers pushed inside and hit what I knew was my prostate and it was all over. I screamed out Tommy's name when my cock erupted like Mt. Vesuvius and jet after jet of cum spurted beneath me.

I couldn't catch my breath and became light-headed. My ass pistoned back onto Tommy's fingers, his fingers repeatedly hit the gland and kept me riding the peak. I heard ringing in my ears. My heart thumped. When Tommy finally removed his fingers, I descended. Exhausted. Sated from the most gripping climax I'd ever had.

He leaned over me and peppered the side of my face with kisses. "So fucking beautiful. I'm going to take you now, Baby. Are you ready?"

I nodded my permission, unable to voice the words. I heard the sound of a packet being ripped and assumed it was a condom. A moment later, I was plied with lube and Tommy's fingers made sure I was coated inside. When the fingers disappeared, I felt the head of his cock at my hole and tensed.

"Relax, Baby."

I slowed my breathing and forced myself to relax. I didn't know this man, but I trusted him to take care of me. He pushed the head of his thick cock through my ring of muscle and I felt the burn and pain of being taken. He paused while I adjusted. When he pushed forward, the pain eased but the delicious burning continued and I couldn't get enough. I lifted my hips and thrust back against him, until he was buried balls deep.

"Fuck, Lee."

We both stilled while I adjusted. Tommy was quivering with tension. I sensed he was afraid of hurting me. When I began moving, causing him to slide in and out, he gripped my hips hard. His nails digging into the soft skin. I didn't care if it left bruises. It was like I'd finally found heaven. Peace. In this man's arms.

He took things slow and I felt a second orgasm building. I'd never come twice in one night in my life. My cock was harder than granite and ached for release. Tommy thrust inside. Harder. Faster. Sweat dripped from our bodies. When he angled himself slightly and hit my prostate, I screamed out his name. Once. Twice. Three times he hammered me and I shattered.

Tommy held me tight against his chest, bit down on the lobe of my ear and I felt the inside of my ass fill with heat. "Fucking hell, Lee. Fuck."

He held me so tight I could barely breathe but we rode out our orgasms together before he withdrew and collapsed onto the bed beside me. Neither of us moved. I'd been thoroughly fucked and I was the happiest I'd ever been in my life.

*** 

After we found the strength, Tommy and I left his bed and showered together. He'd taken both our cocks in hand and while kissing me senseless, managed to draw another orgasm from me. By the time I'd left him - he didn't have to be in at work until four in the afternoon - and headed upstairs to change and go into work, I was worn out. Again. All I'd wanted to do was climb under the covers and sleep the day away. It wasn't a possibility though. One thing my parents had instilled in us kids was, you honored your commitments and obligations.

So, I'd pulled on a pair of jeans, shrugged on a polo shirt and tied my feet into sneakers. The day was warm, the sun bright and I walked with a lightness I hadn't felt in a very long time. Until, thoughts of my past crept in. I wondered if the guilt would ever release its grip. On my way into work, I stopped at a nearby store and purchased the books I'd meant to buy the previous day. I entered the club just before 9am and headed straight to Jake's office. When I stepped inside, I did a double take. The man behind the desk was the image of Jake but with dark hair. They could have just about passed for twins.

"S.sorry," I stammered. "I should have knocked. I didn't expect anyone to be here."

The man stood and moved to shake my hand.

"You must be Lee. My brother told me about you. He said you were gorgeous and would be our big star. He didn't lie about your looks and I imagine he's probably right about you being a star. I'm Roan."

My face heated. I wasn't used to compliments and the man hadn't even seen me on stage yet.

"I'm not sure about being gorgeous or being a star but I am grateful for the opportunity. I was going to work on the books but I can do it later if you're busy." I placed the new books on top of a filing cabinet and started to leave.

"No, it's fine. The meeting I had yesterday was canceled and we're meeting in about thirty minutes. The office is all yours."

Roan removed his suit jacket from the back of the chair he'd been seated in and flung it over one shoulder before heading to the door.

"I'll leave you to it. I should be back in around two."

"Thanks."

I waited for Roan to leave and closed the office door behind him before grabbing everything I needed and flopping into the chair. The sting in my ass as I sat reminded me of what I'd finally done. I smiled in satisfaction. I was hopeful Tommy and I could develop a friends' with benefits relationship like Jake had with Angus.

The thought of Jake caused my cock to flinch and a shiver danced down my spine. What would it be like to be the object of Jake's attraction and thoroughly fucked by the man? I adjusted my jeans to give my semi-hard dick a little more room. I needed to stop fantasizing about my boss, someone I would never be able to have.

\*\*\*

I hadn't realized I'd worked straight through lunch until Roan strolled back into the office. I glanced up at the clock on the wall to find it was almost two. Chris and Pedro had agreed to come in early on the days I worked to continue teaching me the routines. I'd have a couple of hours up on stage with them, until the doors opened at four. I'd then work downstairs with Tommy, out of sight of the patrons, until it was time to head home.

"Have you been at it all day?" Roan asked.

I began closing up the journals I'd be working on and stacked them into a neat pile.

"Yeah, time got away from me. I'm finally starting to see some semblance of order but there's a long way to go."

"You have no idea how thankful we are that Jake found you. I hope once you start on stage, you'll still be able to help us out."

"Of course, I will. Once they're sorted, it won't take long to do the entries each day and I'll have all day Tuesdays and Wednesdays to keep them up to date."

I stood and handed the pile to Roan to stash in the safe.

"If you leave the receipts from each day with them, I'll enter the figures when I come in the following day."

"Have you told Jake?"

I tensed and furrowed my brows. "Have I told Jake what?"

Roan studied me for a moment before speaking. "Have you told Jake to leave the receipts for you?"

"Oh, yes, I did."

Roan nodded.

"Okay, I guess I'll go and wait for Chris and Pedro."

I turned to leave but stopped when Roan spoke again.

"Jake said something is bothering you. I'm here if you'd like to talk."

I stilled with my hand on the door frame. "It's nothing that can be fixed, but thanks."

"Sometimes, it helps to talk things out, Lee. It may not be nearly as bad as you think."

I left the room without another word.

# Chapter Fifteen

**JAKE**

My head pounded when I awoke. Headaches were commonplace lately and there didn't seem to be any reason for them. I resolved to discuss the issue with Roan. I didn't want to start popping pills to mask what could be a problem but I didn't want to trot off to the doctor if it wasn't necessary. Big brother would point me in the right direction like he had done with other issues.

I rolled over and glanced at the clock on the bedside table. The other side of the bed was empty. We'd had an 'energetic' night so I was surprised to find Angus was already up and about. It was only five in the morning.

"You're awake, Sweetheart." Angus padded into the bedroom. He had a tray in his hands containing a teapot, mugs, cream and sugar. Steam wafted from the spout of the teapot. I wasn't a tea drinker but didn't mind one now and again. Angus always drank tea in the morning and I usually joined him if I stayed over.

I rubbed at my face, sat up and dragged fingers through my hair. "Morning. Why the fuck are you always up so early?"

Angus laughed before handing me a mug of tea. After pouring his own, he sat on the edge of the bed.

"What can I say? I'm a morning person."

I massaged the back of my neck, trying to ease some of the throbbing in my head.

"Headache?"

"Yeah. I was just thinking I'd speak with Roan today. See what he recommends."

"I think you need to see a doctor, you get them far too often."

"I don't think it's anything. Stress maybe."

"Just don't ignore them." Angus sipped at his tea. "What's planned for you today?"

"I'm going to head up to the club and see Roan. I want to speak with him about hiring a manager. It will help cut back the hours we're doing. After that, I told Mom and Dad I'd be over. There's a big game on television tonight. The *Packers* are playing the *49ers.* You can bet Dad will be throwing his advice at the *Packers* coach via the television set. There'll be more than a few expletives involved. Mom has plans to visit Aunt Jane."

"Wise move."

"Mom reckons if he was as passionate about mowing the lawns and cleaning out the garage as he is about that team, she wouldn't have to nag."

"She's a woman, she'd find something to give him grief over."

We both laughed and finished our tea in silence. Angus took the mug from my hand and placed a gentle kiss to my forehead.

"Why don't you sleep for a couple of hours. I have some work to do on the computer before I head to work."

I slid back under the covers. "Wake me before you leave?"

"I will."

Angus gathered the tray and padded toward the door, switching the light off and plunging the room into darkness. I closed my eyes and drifted into sleep despite the steady thumping in my head.

***

I entered the club and glanced at the clock on the wall when I noticed Lee was on stage. It was just after three-thirty, the doors wouldn't be open to the public for another half hour. Pedro and Chris were off to one side calling instructions to the young man. I stood watching as he wrapped himself around the pole like a snake before propelling himself into the air in a series of tumbles. He landed on his feet as light as a cat before again sailing through the air and gripping the pole.

"He's good." Roan said from alongside me.

"I can't believe how far he's come in a couple of days. He couldn't even hold himself up when he first started."

Roan stepped in front of me, ensuring I had his full attention. "The customers are going to go wild for him especially when he builds up a bit more muscle. Between the dance training and the workouts with Tommy, it won't take long for his upper body to develop. He's a stunner now, I can only imagine how he'll look in a few weeks. We need to be careful with him. When word gets out, other club owners are going to try and poach him from us and I can guarantee the cops will come sniffing around. We need to hammer into Lee, he can't be on the club floor around the gambling and drinking during opening hours and he's not to be at the bar at any time."

"I know. I've already spoken to him about it. He needs this job and everything that comes with it. He won't get a better deal from the other clubs. I'm not worried."

"He's settled into the apartment?"

"As far as I know. I've been with Angus."

Roan narrowed his eyes.

"Does Angus know you have a thing for the new boy?"

"I don't have a thing for Lee or anyone else. Even if I did, it wouldn't matter. He's seventeen, I'm twenty-six."

"So….."

"So, it's not happening."

"Did you forget there were eleven years between me and Stavros?"

"Yeah and look how that turned out."

"It wasn't our ages that got in the way. He killed the relationship when he cheated on me with an *older* man. Fucking Grant was four years older than me!"

"I know and I'm sorry, but I'm really not interested in Lee. Except as a dancer."

"Keep telling yourself that and maybe the message will reach your dick."

I felt my cheeks heat. I hadn't realized Roan had noticed how hard my cock had become while I'd been watching Lee.

"I need to talk to you. Are you busy?"

"No, I can always spare time for my baby brother. I wondered why you were here on your day off."

I glanced once more at the stage to see Lee was talking with Pedro and Chris. He shot me a quick wave before Roan and I disappeared into the office and closed the door. We both took a seat on the sofa.

"What's on your mind?" Roan asked.

"I think it's time we employed a manager so we can cut back on our hours. It's exhausting me and I know it's doing the same to you."

"I've been having the same thoughts but I don't want to employ someone."

"We can't keep going like we are, Roan."

He lifted his hand. "Hear me out. I'd like to see if Joey is interested in becoming Manager and we can hire on another man to replace him as waiter. I trust Joey and he has proven himself reliable and responsible."

"I like that idea. We'd be employing someone we already know can be trusted. Do you think he'll go for it?"

"He's here, how about we ask him?"

"Okay, but before we do, I have something else to talk to you about."

"Shoot."

"I've been getting a lot of headaches in the past three or four months. My head pounds and at times they're so bad I can barely move with the pain. I don't want to start popping pills. Do you think it could be stress or something more?"

Roan gave me a concerned look. "Does Mom know?"

"Fuck, no. She'd be calling an ambulance and demanding they run every test invented. You know what she's like."

"Good point."

"How often do you get them?"

"Roughly every four or five days. Sometimes they last for a couple of days. I woke up with one again this morning but managed to sleep it off."

"I'm no doctor, Jake, but from the bit of medical training we've both had, I'd say it needs to be checked out. It's probably nothing more than stress or tiredness, but I know I'd feel a lot better if anything serious was ruled out."

"I'll give Dr. Vaughan a call and make an appointment. I just didn't want to take up his time for something trivial. I mean everyone gets headaches now and again."

"Yeah, and if yours were now and again, I wouldn't be concerned but you're getting them far too often. Do you get sick, have trouble with your eyesight when you have one?"

"Almost all the time."

Roan nodded. "You definitely need to see the doctor. Let me know how you go."

"I will. Thanks."

We were interrupted by a knock at the door and Roan opened it to find Joey.

"Just the man we wanted to speak with, come on in."

Roan ushered him in, closed the door and moved to sit behind the desk.

Joey stood waiting, he appeared nervous. "Am I in trouble?"

Roan rushed to assure him. "No, far from it."

"So, what did you need from me?"

"Jake and I are hiring on a manager so we can reduce our hours. We'd like you to take the job."

"Me?"

"You. What do you think?"

Joey held a hand to his chest and shuffled his feet. "I can't believe you're asking me."

"Why shouldn't we? You've proven yourself to be a hard worker, trustworthy and reliable. Will you accept?" I asked.

"I'd be honored."

Roan and I stood and shook hands with the overwhelmed man.

"When would you like me to start?"

"Tomorrow," Roan answered.

"That will leave us a waiter short."

"I'll organise a new waiter and the other men can train him. I'll begin training you tomorrow and we'll work out your hours. You'll work the all-nighters every third Friday and Saturday. Your salary will be increased accordingly," Roan explained.

"I don't know what to say. Thank you both so much."

We both thanked Joey and while he discussed a drink order with Roan, the reason he'd come to the office, I left to head out to Mom and Dad's.

I exited the office and almost collided with Lee who was heading toward the stairs which led down to the dressing room and gym. Tommy was with him and jealousy speared through me when I noted his hand on the small of Lee's back.

"Hi, Jake. I thought it was your day off?" Lee asked.

"It is, I was just leaving. I needed to speak with Roan. Did you get any work done on the books? Don't forget, part of what we pay you is to get them in order and keep them that way. I don't want you up on stage or on the main floor during opening times, we can't afford to get the police offside." Why did I sound so pissed off?

Lee slammed his hands on his bare hips and became defensive at my tone. I can't say I really blamed him. "Yes, I entered everything from yesterday and got quite a lot transferred into the new books. I know I'm not to be out in the main area or on stage when the club is open, you don't need to keep on reminding me. I have no intention of getting you and Roan into trouble or having my ass end up in jail."

Tommy looked back and forth between the two of us, no doubt wondering what the hell was going on.

"As long as you remember. I'll see you in a couple of days."

I stomped off, my headache was back with a vengeance. I felt like an army of drummers was beating a tattoo inside my head.

# Chapter Sixteen

**LIAM**

"What was that about?" Tommy asked as we headed downstairs to the gym.

"No idea. He was obviously pissed about something."

"I've never seen him snap at anyone before, except Rick when he's drunk and refuses to leave. Maybe Roan said something to irritate him."

I shrugged.

"Maybe he didn't like me touching you."

"Why would he care? I mean, we weren't doing anything wrong."

"Maybe he likes you. Maybe he was jealous."

I laughed at that. "Right. I've known him for all of a few hours and you think he's jealous because he likes me. I've never heard such crap."

"Just sayin'. I saw the way he was watching you when you were up on stage. Jake's got a thing for you, my friend."

"Bullshit. You must have deprived your brain of oxygen or something when you worked out."

I stormed into the gym and headed for the change room to pull on a pair of sweats. Tommy followed.

"Maybe *you* have a thing for Jake?"

"Don't be ridiculous, he's my boss!" I jammed my legs into a pair of sweats and headed to a treadmill to work off some of the annoyance and to warm up.

Tommy jumped onto the machine next to me. Before we could argue further, Sam sauntered in.

"Did you hear Joey's to start as manager tomorrow night?" Sam started up the machine on the other side of Tommy and they fell into conversation.

My thoughts drifted to Jake. I was puzzled as to why he'd become angry, I'd certainly given him no reason to be. Could Tommy be right? Nah, there was no way Jake could be interested in me. We'd only just met for fuck sake. Could he be regretting hiring me? Was he going to tell me it was all a big mistake and I was fired?

"Lee!"

I jolted myself free from my thoughts when Sam shouted my name.

"Yes?"

"I just asked you twice – how's the dancing going? I caught the tail end of your routine and it looks fantastic. Pedro and Chris have outdone themselves."

"I think I'm getting the hang of it but I still falter when my arms tire."

"Tommy said you've started strength training so that will help."

"I hope so. I don't particularly want to make a fool of myself by falling flat on my face the first time I get up there. More importantly, I don't want to betray everyone's faith in me."

"Trust me, you won't make a fool of yourself if the little I saw was an example. You'll blow them away. They won't be interested in us after seeing you."

"Right, like that'll happen. I'll never be as good as the rest of you."

Sam turned to Tommy. "We can't complain about him having a huge ego like Dixon." To me he said, "You have no idea how good you are. You're a natural, Lee."

***

Tommy was like a fucking Sargent Major when it came to my training. He didn't give an inch and demanded I perfect every move. The man was relentless. By the time we were done, my arms and legs felt like noodles. I'd barely been able to put one foot in front of the other earlier today and I knew it would get a whole lot worse before it got better. My muscles were gonna hurt like a sonofabitch tomorrow.

"Hit the shower."

They were the best words I'd heard come out of his mouth for the past hour and a half. Until, he reminded me it needed to be cold.

"Fuck off!" I snarled at him before grabbing a fresh change of clothes from a locker I'd been allocated and stomping along to the shower block. As I reached out to open the door to a stall, he grabbed my arm and spun me around to face him.

"What's with the fucking attitude?"

"I'm tired, pissed off that you think there's some attraction between Jake and I and pissed with how Jake spoke to me."

"That's fine, but don't go taking it out on the rest of us. We look out for each other here, we're honest and don't take offense when the truth is pointed out. I believe you and Jake are attracted to each other and you need to get it sorted out before it affects everyone else here."

Before I could respond, Tommy entered the stall next to me and slammed the door. While I showered, I thought about what he'd said. I had been a prick. Maybe Jake and I needed to sit down and have an honest conversation. I couldn't deny what Tommy had said, I was attracted to my boss. Could we have a relationship like the one he had with Angus? There was no doubt in my mind, it could never be anything more serious.

By the time I finished showering – yes, a cold, fucking shower – and dressed, Tommy was gone. He was dancing tonight so the first place I checked for him was the dressing room. Chris and Pedro, Sam and Dixon were there but there was no sign of Tommy.

"Do you know where Tommy is?"

"What did you do to upset him? He's gone upstairs." Sam raised an eyebrow while the other men fixed me with a stare.

"I disagreed with something he said and got pissy. I can't go upstairs, can one of you go and ask him if we can talk, please?"

"I'm here, say what you have to. I need to get ready to go on stage."

I spun around at the sound of Tommy's voice, I hadn't heard him move up behind me.

"I'm sorry. I'll give him a call and ask if I can talk with him tomorrow, try and get it sorted."

Tommy nodded.

"What's going on?" Dixon asked.

"Jake and I are attracted to each other and it caused some tension earlier," I admitted.

"Finally." Pedro and Chris's eyes locked. "We knew from the moment they met, didn't we, Chris."

"I've never seen Jake's eyes sparkle like they do when Lee's in the room. There's definitely something," Chris agreed.

Pedro scooted his chair across the floor to where Chris sat applying makeup and laid his head on his shoulder. "True love. I wonder when their wedding will be?"

I sighed. I'd come to work with a bunch of delusional romantics.

"Guys, aren't you getting a little ahead of yourselves? I admit, there is something, I'm not sure exactly what, but we barely know each other. I have no intention of getting into a serious relationship with him or anyone else regardless of how we might feel. I'm not worthy of love and never will be. I don't deserve to be alive. Accepting this job might have been a mistake. You're all too good for me to be around. Night."

I didn't wait for questions as to why I'd said what I had. As I left the club, I realized I'd spoken the truth. I didn't belong around these men. I wondered if maybe there was a liquor store nearby, one where they wouldn't ask too many questions. Making friends with a bottle of tequila sounded like a great idea right about now.

*** 

I'd been fortunate to find a liquor store half a block from the club. It was situated in a side street, the only indication it was there – a green light stating it was *Viper's One Stop Liquor Shop*. If the light hadn't caught my eye, I wouldn't have known anything about it. The street appeared to be a hangout for prostitutes and drug dealers. I ignored the comments thrown my way from a very tall person slouched in a doorway, they made it clear they wanted a quick fuck for money.

I slipped into the shop. The man behind the counter was intimidating and had he asked for ID, I would have hightailed it out of the place. He wasn't as tall as me but was built like a proverbial brick wall. His biceps bulged from under the sleeves of the shirt he wore and were as large as the tops of my thighs. He had some impressive ink which I couldn't help but admire. I wondered how Jake and Roan would feel about their dancers having tattoos and remembered, both Tommy and Sam had a couple.

Fortunately, the man-wall didn't ask me any questions. I handed him the money and he thrust the bottle at me. He didn't bother concealing the purchase with a brown paper bag. I left the store, hurried from the street and headed toward the building where I currently lived. I'd spend another night in the place before moving on. To where, I wasn't sure.

I entered the apartment, kicked the door shut and flopped on the sofa. I opened the bottle and gulped down a mouthful of the smooth liquid. Despite what my brother thought, I didn't drink alcohol on many occasions. When things began to close in on me, I usually resorted to wiping myself out. I knew I had issues and needed help but I couldn't seem to get past my self-hatred.

I took another swig from the bottle and switched on the television set. It was connected to cable and would have the porn channel, but I just didn't feel in the mood. I found a channel showing an old black and white movie and settled back to watch while I drank. It didn't take long for me to start feeling the effects of the potent liquid and I found myself falling into a deep depression.

Visions of the past..... Steve being wheeled from the building on a gurney, the side of his head black and swollen, filled my head. Paramedics telling Mom and Dad, it was a serious head injury. I'll never forget the way my parents looked at me when I'd confessed to helping Josh.

I set the almost empty bottle on the floor and stumbled through to the bathroom to relieve myself. The disposable razor sat on the sink. Mocking me. Daring me. I accepted the challenge. Picking up the razor, I broke the blade away from the plastic and climbed into the bathtub. I didn't want to leave a mess which would be hard to clean up. Tears filled my eyes, pity for myself at knowing what I'd so stupidly thrown away. I knew now, there was no going back.

I sliced the blade over my wrist, pushing it deep into the muscle. Making sure I didn't make the same mistake as last time. Blood flowed from the wound. I sliced at the other wrist before placing the blade on the side of the bath and laying my head back.

"I'm sorry, Mom. Dad. Steve. I love you all."

I heard a vague knocking sound but was too drowsy to bother worrying about where it was coming from. The blood flowed from my wrists, soaking my shirt and pants. I closed my eyes and waited for the darkness of death to gather me in its arms.

"Holy fuck! Call 911 and Jake." It was Tommy's voice.

*Too late*, was the last thought I had before I felt my heart slow and darkness engulf me.

***

## JAKE

"**F**or fuck sake. A six-year-old kid could run faster than him. PICK YOUR FUCKING FEET UP AND RUN!"

I chuckled as Dad yelled at the television set. His beloved 49ers were down by five points and time was running out. If the game didn't end soon, I was sure he was going to have a coronary. Thankfully, my headache was gone although with the blasting of the television and Dad's shouting, I was surprised it hadn't returned. I felt my phone buzz in my pocket and frowned. It was almost midnight. Who the hell would be calling me at this time of night?

I frowned when Jenkins' name flashed on the screen. I pushed the button to connect.

"Jenkins?"

"Boss, you need to get to County right away."

My heart jumped into my throat. I leapt to my feet and grabbed the car keys from the small table in front of me.

"What's going on?"

"It's Lee, looks like he won't make it."

"Fuck!"

Dad stood and placed a hand on my shoulder.

"I'll be there in twenty."

I disconnected the call. "Dad, I have to go. One of our dancers is in the hospital."

"Is he okay?"

"Doesn't sound like it. I don't know what happened, he was fine when I saw him this afternoon."

Dad walked me to the car. "Drive carefully and call me when you know something. I hope he's okay."

"Thanks, Dad. I'll let you know when I find out something."

He stood in the light of the front porch as I reversed the car from the driveway and turned toward the city. Tears burned my eyes. Jenkins had said Lee wouldn't make it. What the fuck had happened? Had he been hit by a car? Beaten up on his way home? Fallen? I needed him to be okay. I drove a little faster than I should have but at this time of night the streets were quiet. I made good time to County, parked the car and hurried through the doors to Emergency.

I rushed up to a woman behind a glass window. "Liam Masters, I'm his emergency contact – Jake Brown. Where is he?"

"Mr. Brown, we've been expecting you. Level 3. Let the nurse at the desk know who you are. Dr. Davies would like to speak with you."

"Is Liam okay?"

"Sir, I'm sorry but I'm unable to give you any further information."

"Please, I need to know if he's alive."

"Sir, please speak with Dr. Davies."

My stomach turned over with dread and nausea washed over me. I turned and raced for the elevator. Thankfully, it was on the ground floor and the doors opened immediately. I stepped inside and pushed the button for the third level. The fucking thing seemed to take forever to reach the floor I needed. When the doors opened and I stepped out, I saw Jenkins and Tommy sitting in chairs off to my left. Tommy's face was pale, his eyes red from crying. I hurried over to them.

"What happened? Is he okay?"

"He tried to kill himself and came too fucking close to succeeding. If I hadn't thought to check on him on my way home, he'd be lying in his apartment – dead."

I was confused and terrified. "He tried to kill himself? How? Why?"

"He sliced his wrists with a razor. I found him in the bathtub. Blood was everywhere. He lost so much blood, Jake. I thought he was already gone but I felt a weak pulse. While I wrapped towels around his wrists to try and stop the bleeding, Jenkins called 911. The Paramedics arrived about five minutes later. They brought him straight here. I don't know where he is or what they're doing. We were told to wait here and someone would speak with us once you arrived."

"Why did he do it? I thought everything was going okay."

"So did I. We were together last night and he seemed happy, but something he said before he left the club bothered me which is why I wanted to check on him."

"What did he say?"

"He said he wasn't worthy of love and didn't deserve to be alive. He thought taking the job was a mistake."

I dragged my fingers through my hair and paced the floor. "Something happened before he came here. Something involving someone called, Steve. I tried to get him to talk to me but all he'd say was that he'd done something unforgiveable but it wasn't illegal. What the fuck could he have done that would want to make him kill himself?"

"He didn't say anything to me last night or this morning, but then again, I didn't exactly ask."

I narrowed my eyes at Tommy. "You were together all night?"

"We had dinner and he fell asleep watching a movie. When I woke him, he didn't want to go home. I offered him the guest room but he fell asleep in the bathroom when he went to brush his teeth. My bedroom was closest so, I put him in my bed with me. He's not exactly a lightweight and it was as far as I could manage to carry him."

I felt rage build inside. "Did you fuck?"

Tommy dropped his head and I was gripped with hurt. I'd known Lee was a virgin and I'd wanted to be his first. I shook my head at my self-absorbed attitude. Who the fuck did I think I was. Lee had every right to fuck whoever he wanted. Right now, I needed to focus on how we could best help him.

"Mr. Brown?"

I swung around at the sound of my voice to find a man in a white coat approaching.

"Yes." I held out my hand and we shook.

"I'm Geoff Davies, come through to my office." He held his arm out indicating a door opposite where we stood.

Tommy and Jenkins stepped to my side.

"I'd like these two men to hear what you have to say, they're the ones who found him."

When Dr. Davies nodded, the men stepped forward and shook hands, introducing themselves.

The room he led us into had a pair of sofas and a small table. We all sat.

"Mr. Masters is in surgery having the damage to his wrists repaired before he's stitched up. He doesn't appear to have done anything major that will restrict the use of his hands but it will be a month or so before he can use them normally."

I let out a deep sigh of relief.

"He lost a lot of blood and if you men had been five minutes later, you'd be arranging a funeral. We'll keep him here for a day or so and replace the blood he lost. I'll also schedule him to speak with a Psychiatrist. Do you have any idea why he'd do this?"

"There's something in his past. He refuses to talk about it but it's obviously tearing him apart," I answered.

"Does he have family?"

I didn't want to lie, but I did so for Lee's sake. "No, which is why I'm his emergency contact. I'm actually his employer."

The doctor paused and appeared to be thinking. "I think he should be sent to a Psychiatric Hospital, at least until we can be sure he's no longer suicidal and a danger to himself. I'd like to start him on medication also."

"No. Absolutely not. Both my brother and I are trained Psychologists. I'll take him home with me and get him to open up. You're not going to drug him out until he resembles a zombie and a hospital would only make things worse."

"You haven't managed to get him to confide in you up to now." The doctor's barb stung.

"He will, we just need time."

"You may not have time, Mr. Brown. This was an extremely serious attempt to end his life and came within a breath of succeeding."

"I'll take care of him. I assure you, we'll take every precaution so it doesn't happen again."

"Very well. I'll still get the Psych. eval. though. It's legal procedure in these circumstances."

"Yes, I know. When will he be out of surgery?"

The doctor checked the watch at his wrist. "In about thirty minutes. If you wait here, I'll send someone for you when you can see him."

We all stood, shook hands and the doctor left the room.

# Chapter Seventeen

**LIAM**

My eyes flickered open and I glanced around. Tears filled my eyes. I'd failed again. I was still alive. Jake appeared to be dozing in a chair which was pulled close to one side of the bed. On the other side, Tommy and Jenkins were seated and snoring softly.

"Jake?" My voice was soft, hoarse.

Jake shot upright in his chair and leaned toward me. "You're awake. How do you feel?"

"How did I get here?"

"Tommy and Jenkins found you. They called the Paramedics and me. We need to talk, Lee, but I want you to rest."

"I don't want to talk about it. Why couldn't they leave me? Let me die."

Jake covered my hand with his. I glanced down and noted the thick white bandages around both wrists. "We care about you, Lee."

"You don't know me. You don't know what I've done. If you did, I'd be dead now." Anger welled within and tears rolled over my cheeks. "I can't keep going, Jake. I just can't do it anymore."

Jake sat on the side of the bed and drew me into his arms. I sobbed into his chest.

"I hate myself and you should too."

Jake ran one hand over my head and the other over my back as he held me close. I'd never felt more cared about.

"Honey, nothing is so bad that you need to kill yourself over it. You need to start trusting in someone to help you through this. I hoped it would be me but you can speak with Roan if you prefer. The doctor we spoke with said he was sending a Psychiatrist to evaluate you tomorrow, today actually. It's five in the morning. He thought you should be sent to a hospital for a while."

I pushed out of Jake's arms. "Please, don't let that happen, Jake. Please, I couldn't bear to be in a place like that."

"I told him you're coming home with me and I'd watch over you, get to the bottom of what's going on."

"Home with you? Why?"

"I care about you, Lee. I've felt something special from the first time I set eyes on you. When I saw Tommy's hand on your back yesterday, I suspected you'd been together and it made me crazy with jealousy. I'm sorry I snapped at you."

"I'm so confused, Jake. I hurt so much." I lowered my head back to his chest and he wrapped his arms around me.

"I know, Honey. We'll figure it out, I give you my word."

Somehow, I knew Jake would make things better for me and I resolved at that time, to place my full trust in him.

\*\*\*

"How are you feeling?" The nurse asked when she breezed into the room.

Tommy and Jenkins had left an hour earlier, needing to get into work. They confided that their boss was an unbending jerk who wouldn't understand they'd spent the night watching over a friend. We'd all had a good laugh over that. Jake had told them to call Roan and ask him to organize for others to take their places but they insisted they'd be able to work. I thanked them for what they'd done and apologized for worrying them. They both informed me, it's what friends did – they looked out for each other.

"I'm fine. Am I able to go home?"

"Not until Dr. Winters has spoken with you. If he's satisfied you'll be safe, he'll sign the release papers."

I nodded and glanced at Jake who smiled reassuringly and gathered my hand in his. After the nurse left, I relaxed back against the pillows.

"Would you like me to call your family?"

A cold shiver galloped through me. I doubted my parents would care. Why did thinking that hurt so badly?

"No. I don't want them to know anything about me and I doubt they'd want to know."

Before Jake could try and convince me otherwise, a man in a white coat entered the room.

"Liam, how are you doing? My name is Dale Winters. I'm a Psychiatrist and I'd like to have a chat with you."

"Can Jake stay, please?"

The doctor nodded at Jake who squeezed my hand. "Of course, if that's what you prefer."

"Thank you." I dreaded what might come next.

The doctor moved closer to the head of the bed, he held a file in his hands.

"Would you like to tell me why you tried to take your own life?"

I sighed. "I didn't feel like I had the right to be alive, to be happy."

"Why not?"

"Because of something I did."

"Did you kill someone?"

"No, but I helped someone who did."

"So, you were present and helped someone kill another person?"

"No."

"I'm confused. You helped someone to kill but you weren't present and you're not in jail."

"No."

"Would you care to explain how that's possible?"

I shot a quick glance at Jake who had a puzzled expression on his face.

"I'd rather not talk about it."

"I can't release you unless I'm convinced you're safe. I can't be convinced if I don't know what is troubling you."

"Please, I give you my word, I'll talk with Jake when I leave here."

I was trembling, terrified of ending up in a Psychiatric hospital. I'd heard about those places and some of the things that were done there. If I had to, I would confess everything but I wanted to confide in Jake, not some stranger who really didn't care about me. To him, I was only a job. A patient number.

"I'm a qualified Trauma Psychologist," Jake explained.

"I'm advised that Liam will be going home under your supervision?"

"Yes, he will be. As one professional to another, I guarantee you; if I so much as suspect Lee will try this again, I'll contact you for advice. I'll make sure to give you a weekly update. I don't feel a hospital is in Lee's best interest at this time, but if it becomes necessary, I won't hesitate to recommend he be placed in one."

I snapped my eyes to Jake's, there was no doubt he was deadly serious.

"Very well." The doctor turned his attention back to me. "I will sign the release papers, but if you leave Jake's home before we agree, I will contact the police and you *will* be taken to hospital."

"I understand." That put an end to my plan to abscond at the first opportunity. Nope, I would have to come clean and deal with Jake's disgust. Maybe it was my penance?

***

Jake held the door open and I stepped into his apartment. The place was incredible but I was too preoccupied to really appreciate it.

"Have a seat. Coffee?"

"No, thanks."

"Water, soda?"

"Water, thanks."

Jake grabbed two bottles of water, placed them on a small table and sat beside me. He tucked one leg under the other so he was facing me, I did the same. When he attempted to gather my hands in his, I pulled back.

"Talk to me, Lee. I promise, it will stay between us and I won't judge."

I sighed deeply and fisted my hands in my lap.

"I'll give you the short version of my life so you understand why I did what I did a bit better."

"I'm listening."

"I grew up with everything. My parents are incredibly wealthy and we wanted for nothing. Mom and Dad met in a restaurant. Mom inherited a lot of money and was super rich. Dad hated her but she decided she wanted him and she always got what she wanted. They fell in love, married and they had me less than a year later. I have two sisters who are younger. I also have an older brother – well, adopted brother, Steve."

Jake nodded.

"Steve lived in the 'hood, a particularly seedy part of town, where dad had an apartment before he was married. Steve's mother was a prostitute, drug addict and alcoholic. Dad had grown up in a similar situation and he felt sorry for Steve so he took him under his wing. The only meals he had were those Dad made for him or leftovers from the restaurant where he worked. When Steve's mother overdosed, Dad took him to live with him. When my parents married, they adopted him."

"Steve was special and you felt you were missing out."

"Yeah. He was good at everything he did. Following him through school was a fucking nightmare. Teachers constantly compared us in everything – grades, sports, drama, music. Nothing I did was good enough. So, I rebelled. I was constantly disobedient, causing trouble. When I reached high school, I started cutting class and hanging out in the 'hood. I tried alcohol and the first time I went home drunk; Mom and Dad went ballistic. The more they rode me, the wilder

I became. After one argument I had with my father he asked me while I'd become so wild. I told him I was born to be wild. I was grounded, forced to stay with Uncle Wade and Uncle Rafe when the rest of the family went on family holidays and missed out on special outings. My uncles tried to talk to me as well but it fell on deaf ears."

I paused and took a mouthful of water.

"I was jealous of Steve. The more he achieved, the more I seemed to fail. I wanted our parents to be as proud of me as they were of him. When Steve graduated college with almost perfect results, Dad threw a party for him and it was the beginning of the end for me."

"What happened?"

"He announced to all our family and friends that he was proud Steve would inherit the family business one day, at least it would be in trustworthy hands. He was staring straight at me when he said it. I was fifteen at the time. I stormed out of the party and didn't go home for two days. When I did go home, they went on and on about how ungrateful I was, how much trouble I was."

"They were probably worried sick and angry."

I nodded.

"Steve started working in the 'hood, helping people find jobs and doing lots of stuff for them. He met a woman called Keegan. She was in an abusive relationship and he helped her get away. When he told my parents about her, they almost fell over themselves in worshipping him for being such a good person. It was sickening. I hated him. I hated all of them."

"You felt left out."

"I *was* left out. Anyway, I got talking to a guy in a bar one afternoon....."

"A bar?"

"In the 'hood no-one cares if you're underage. So, this guy was telling me how some guy had helped his woman to leave him and she owed him a heap of money. He was really angry. I started complaining about how my brother had saved some woman and my parents thought he was fucking God. I might as well have been invisible for all they cared about me. After moaning for a while, we figured out we were talking about the same woman. I agreed to help him get her back. I knew Steve had feelings for Keegan and I wanted him to hurt when she disappeared. I cut class the next day and followed Steve and Keegan to their apartment. I hung around out the front and called Josh to tell him where they were. He arrived at the building and went inside. I didn't go with him because I didn't want Steve to know it was me who'd given Josh the information. While I was waiting, Mom and

Dad turned up. They were carrying a trash bag and I found out later they were dropping some clothes off for Keegan. Mom used her key to go inside, they found Steve and called for an ambulance. The Paramedics arrived and Steve was brought out on a gurney. I raced over to him, terrified he was dead. He was unconscious, his face was bruised and he was bleeding. Josh had knocked him out using the butt of his gun. He could have been killed. I went to the hospital with Mom while Dad went in the ambulance. I confessed what I'd done to her on the way."

"What about Keegan?"

"I didn't see her and Josh leave the building and I found out later that Josh had taken her out the back exit. He drove her to his apartment. Mom called Steve's business partner and he knew where Keegan had lived before Steve had intervened. He gave her the address and she called the cops. By the time the police arrived, Keegan was close to death. Josh had beaten her to within an inch of her life and left her to die. The hospital didn't expect her to pull through but thankfully she did. Her and Steve would be married now. Dad refused to speak to me over the next few days, he couldn't stand the sight of me. He couldn't understand how one of his sons could turn so viciously on the other. My sisters hated me and one said she disowned me. Mom barely said a word. I despised myself for what I'd done and knew every time they looked at me, it would remind them of what had happened. So, I left. I lived on the streets of Linton for a couple of nights until a Chinese lady found me and took me in. She paid for me to go to college to learn Accounting and I worked in her restaurant so I could pay the rent on a seedy apartment I lived in. It was going well."

"Why did you leave there if it was working out?"

"Steve found me and wanted me to go home. I couldn't do it and because he knew where I was, he wouldn't have left me alone. He said he forgave me and so did Keegan but I didn't believe him."

"So, you ran and ended up here."

"Yes."

"I don't understand. You said someone was killed?"

I nodded. "Keegan was pregnant with Josh's baby. She lost it when he beat her."

Jake sat quietly, his eyes lowered.

"Now you know the whole sordid story. Now you know why I should be dead."

His head snapped up.

"Lee, you were young. A teenager who didn't think that what you were doing would get anyone hurt. You had no way of knowing what Josh would do. Was what you did wrong? Yes, it was. Do you deserve to be hated or dead? Absolutely not. One of the things I learned when I studied psychology are that teenagers are a self-absorbed bunch who tend to exaggerate situations. You felt left out, jealous of your brother and some of it may have been justified. Your wild behavior was a cry for attention but it was misinterpreted. Your parents saw it as you behaving like an entitled brat."

"I was a prick. I'd had everything, Jake, from birth. Steve ate out of the fucking trash. He had no shoes, had to look after a mother who didn't care if he lived or died. He wanted to excel at everything he did so Mom and Dad didn't regret adopting him. I can see that now. I just wish it wasn't too late. I love them all so much and I really miss home."

"Why don't you go and speak with them? It sounds like Steve is ready to have you back if he came looking for you."

"I can't, Jake. How could they ever forgive me? I couldn't live with seeing the hate in Dad's eyes every time I looked at him. It's one of the reasons I needed to leave."

Jake pulled me into his arms when tears began rolling down my cheeks. He kissed the top of my head. When he eased me back, he placed a hand to each side of my face.

"Why did you try to kill yourself? I thought you were happy at the club. The other men like you."

"I like them all but I was getting too close, becoming friends. Spending time with them. Laughing, joking. I was scared."

"Of what?"

"Scared you'd find out about me and hate me like my family does. I couldn't handle it. I don't want to keep moving. Running. But I couldn't risk any of you knowing my secret."

"Then, don't run. Stay here with people who care about you. I won't tell you to go home, you can only do that when you're ready. And, when you are, I'll be by your side."

"You don't hate me?"

"Of course, I don't. We have a lot to talk about but we both need sleep. How about we go to bed for a while?"

I took Jake's proffered hand and stood. I felt like the weight of the world had been lifted from my shoulders. That I'd been re-born.

Whatever happened from here, Jake would be there for me to talk to.

# Chapter Eighteen

**LIAM**

Someone was running their hand through my hair and the sensation caused goosebumps to break out over my skin. I opened my eyes to find Jake sitting beside the bed watching me. I remembered where I was and what had happened.

"Hi," Jake said. "How are you feeling?"

"My arms feel like a truck ran over them but I guess it serves me right. How long was I asleep?"

"About five hours. Are you hungry?"

"A little."

"How about I order take out? Do you feel like coming out to the living room for a while, we can talk?"

I nodded. Jake stood and helped me from the bed. Once I was standing, he wrapped me in a soft robe to cover the boxer briefs I was wearing. Taking my hand, he led me out to the living room and I sat on the sofa which faced a set of glass doors. There were spectacular views over the harbor. The sun was low in the sky and a plethora of colors cascaded on the horizon.

I glanced around the rest of the apartment. The place was enormous. It was decorated in shades of blue, accented with white.

"This is a nice place. Have you been here long?"

"About a year. We moved in not long after the building was completed."

Silence sat heavy between us, I sensed there was something Jake wanted to say and was nervous about saying it. I twisted my fingers together. My palms felt clammy.

"Jake...."

"Lee...."

We'd spoken at almost the same time.

"You first," I said.

"I don't know what's happening but ever since I laid eyes on you, I can't keep you out of my mind. You've been in my thoughts every second of every day. I want to go into the club even on my days off when I know you're there. When Tommy called me to tell me what you'd done, it broke my heart. I was terrified you wouldn't make it. I was furious at myself for the way I'd spoken to you earlier in the day."

"I'm sorry."

"You're okay and that's all that matters. Lee, I know I'm too old for you. We're all like a family at the club, not like normal employer and employees but the fact remains, I'm your boss for fuck sake. I'm not supposed to get involved with someone who works for me. Problem is, no matter how much I tell myself that, it makes no fucking difference. My brain is saying one thing, my heart – another. I can't fight this attraction and I want to give us a go. I want us to date, spend some time together."

"I want that too."

"You do?"

"Yes, I do. I have no idea where what we feel will lead us, but I want to find out."

Jake beamed, pulled me into his arms and his lips crashed down on mine. Our lips brushed. Tongues tested one another out. Teeth nipped. It was the best kiss I'd ever had. Better than I'd imagined. I wrapped my arms around Jake's waist and clung to him as if my life depended on it. Every nerve in my body came to life. I felt like I now had a reason to go on living.

We pulled apart to catch our breath and I ran a hand over Jake's stubbled cheek. "You're not too old for me, you're just right."

"I want you so bad, but it's not happening - *yet*. I want to do this right. Wine and dine you.

Take you dancing. Get to know each other and make sure it's what we both want." Jake held my hands in his.

"I'd like that."

"First off, we need to get you healed so you can go back home and get back to work. You're my star and I need you to be ready when I present you to the world."

"Did the doctor say if there would be any permanent damage or weakness?"

"He said you should regain full use and strength in both hands. I guess time will tell but he didn't seem to think you would have any problems."

I breathed a sigh of relief.

"When can I go home and back to work?"

"You can come into work tomorrow if you feel up to working on the books. There's to be no training though. Home? Maybe in a week if I'm satisfied with your state of mind."

"I'll go into the club but it's gonna be hard facing the others. Am I able to do some running on the treadmill? I don't want my fitness to suffer."

"The other men will hover over you after this. They'll be concerned and worried for you but they won't judge. I can't see why you can't do anything that doesn't involve your hands. No strength or pole training for at least two weeks though. I'll get the doctor to check and make sure everything is okay before you start again."

"Fair enough. If you won't fuck me, will you at least feed me?"

Jake laughed, kissed the tip of my nose and reached for the phone to place the order.

***

We were almost finished a feast of Thai food when a knock came at the door. Jake stood, padded across the room and opened the door. Roan stood on the other side.

"Come on in."

Roan smiled at me as he entered and sat on the sofa facing us. Jake resumed his seat beside me.

"Want something to eat?" Jake asked.

"No, I just wanted to check in on Lee." He turned his attention to me. "How are you feeling?"

"I'll be fine. I'm sorry I caused so much trouble for everyone."

Roan shook his head. "You didn't cause trouble. We were worried about you and concerned that we hadn't foreseen what you were going to do. If Tommy hadn't been troubled by what you'd said, fuck knows what could have happened. I'm glad he found you in time."

"Thanks," I mumbled.

"Have you talked?" Roan asked his brother.

"Yes, we had a long talk this afternoon. I'm glad you're here. There's something else you need to know."

Roan lifted an eyebrow.

"Lee and I are going to start seeing each other. We feel an attraction and want to see where it leads."

"That news won't surprise anyone. We could all see there was something pulling you together. I hope it works out but like everyone else has to, keep your dick in your pants at the club."

"We will, but that's a ways off yet. First we're going to date."

Roan stood. "I'm glad you appear to be doing okay, Lee. Remember, there's absolutely nothing you can't talk to us about."

"Thanks, Roan."

He let himself out

"He'll let the other men know you're with me. It will set their minds at ease."

"I don't deserve all of y……"

Jake placed his warm fingers gently over my lips to silence me.

"I don't want to hear talk like that ever again. I think you're a good man who made an error in judgement. We've all done it, Lee. There are very few mistakes which need to be paid for with the rest of our lives and what you did isn't one of them. I want you to focus on forgiving yourself."

"I'll try."

Jake leaned forward and kissed me. A gentle kiss at first but then it deepened and took my breath away.

I wanted this man more than I'd ever wanted anything. When we parted and he sat back, I studied his eyes. They were dark with passion, lust.

"Jake, please take me to bed."

"Are you tired? Do you feel ill?"

I gathered his hand. "I feel fucking amazing after that kiss. Take me to bed, Jake."

"But....."

I placed my fingers over his lips and the protest died.

"No, buts. I need you."

Jake nodded, stood and gathered my hand. We headed to the bedroom without saying another word. My dick danced in my briefs.

*\*\**

Jake stood me beside the bed, unfastened the tie on the robe, slid it off my shoulders and it floated to the floor. I trembled in anticipation. Taking my face in his hands, he kissed me. It wasn't urgent but I sensed the deep passion. Soft kisses were placed over my face and when he moved to the area between my shoulder and neck, I tilted my head to the side, giving him better access to the soft skin.

Ripples raced through every nerve and I shuddered slightly. Jake dropped to his knees and his hands molded over my brief covered ass. I rested my hands on his wide shoulders and gasped when his mouth latched onto a nipple. He tugged and nipped, licked and kissed before starting on the other tight bud. I could feel my dick weeping, the briefs becoming damp. My moans broke into the silence of the room.

Slowly, he descended my body, placing featherlight kisses all over my skin. I could feel my legs starting to shake. When Jake sucked my dick through the fabric of my briefs, I almost sank to the floor. My mind clouded with pleasure. A myriad of sensation bombarded every cell. I pushed closer to Jake's mouth and when he

242

moved back, I could have cried with disappointment. He pushed the briefs to my ankles, I stepped out of them and he tossed them aside.

"Exquisite," Jake murmured before taking me into his mouth.

He suctioned the head of my cock like a human vacuum cleaner before pushing further onto my length. I felt the tip of my cock hit the back of his throat before he relaxed and took me in deeper. I was squeezed hard and when he groaned around me, my knees buckled. Jake wrapped his hands around my waist, it was all that was holding me up. His tongue danced along my dick. His mouth twisted, sucked. I could feel an orgasm building. Pre-cum leaked from me like my dick was a faucet. Jake hummed around me. My fingers pulled at his hair and I thrust my hips back and forth.

"Jake, I'm going to come."

He gazed up at me with watery eyes and nodded. I expected him to pull away but when he didn't, I placed a hand on his head to push him back. He pushed against me, refusing to let go. His sucking became firmer, more insistent. My balls tingled and I yelled out his name as I emptied into his throat. I could barely remember my own name as the orgasm was drawn out by Jake's talented mouth.

When my legs shook out of control, Jake released me, lifted me into his arms and lay me onto the bed. I watched as he quickly stripped and rolled on a condom. Every inch of his body was perfection, I had no idea why he wasn't up on stage. He certainly had the build to outrival any of us. His dick wasn't quite the length of Tommy's but he was much thicker. I hoped I could take all of him.

When he crawled onto the bed, I attempted to roll onto my belly but Jake placed a hand on my hip and stopped me.

"I want to look into your eyes as you come apart for me."

I settled onto my back and spread my legs.

Jake pushed my legs back against my chest, leaving me fully exposed.

"Fucking gorgeous."

His head disappeared between my legs and I jumped when I felt his tongue at my hole. The click of the cap on the bottle of lube sounded and moments later, a long finger pushed inside me. I relaxed and pushed against it. Two fingers. Then, three. I circled my hips, my body writhed. I needed more. Needed him deeper.

The fingers and his mouth disappeared and I felt him settle his cock at my entrance. Slowly he inched into me. The pain faded to burning as he sank deeper. Once fully seated, he lowered his body to mine, my dick sandwiched between us and we kissed deeply. I could taste myself on his tongue. In his mouth. Sweet with a bitter edge. I forced my hips to lift against his weight and he broke the kiss.

"Anxious, are we?"

"Please, Jake. You're fucking killing me."

Jake laughed before sliding out and thrusting back in. I held his ass cheeks in my hands so he couldn't escape me, being mindful of my injured wrists.

With every hard thrust, I lifted to meet it head on. Tingles radiated from my balls, shot down my legs to my toes. My leaking dick was harder than concrete. I couldn't risk sliding a hand between us to jerk myself off for fear the pounding I was receiving would tear open the stitches. Sweat trickled from Jake's forehead and landed on my face. As a monumental orgasm approached, I thrashed beneath him. Tore at his back with my nails – thoughts of my injuries now gone. When Jake twisted his hips and hit the prostate, it was all over. I screamed his name over and over as I emptied against both of our stomachs. Seconds later, Jake came with a roar. He held me so tight I could barely breathe. What exquisite torture. Together, we rode out our orgasms. Jake bit at my neck. Smothered my face with kisses. I felt the warmth of his semen filled condom in my now sensitive ass.

I clung to him, never wanting to let go. A tear slid from my eye. In my heart I knew, I'd found where I belonged. Who I belonged with.

Jake slid out of me, padded to the bathroom and disposed of the condom. He returned with a warm wash cloth, cleaned me up and tossed it to the floor before climbing back into the bed. Reaching over, he rolled me into his arms, my head resting on his chest. One arm draped over his waist. A soft kiss caressed my forehead.

"So much for dating and getting to know each other before we started fucking," Jake said with a wry grin." You know there's no way I'll leave you alone now, don't you?"

"I don't mind."

"I'm sure you don't. Just remember when you're begging me for five minutes of sleep, you started it."

"Fair enough." I lifted my head and brushed my lips over Jake's. "Goodnight, Jake, thank you for everything."

I settled back into the warmth of his body and drifted into sleep.

# Chapter Nineteen

*Five months later*

"Happy Birthday, Honey."

Jake lifted my chin from where it rested on his ribs and crashed his lips against mine. I pushed him onto his back and rolled on top of him. Our aroused cocks slid together, both hard as steel. My hands tugged at his hair. He moaned into my mouth while his hands explored my back and caressed my ass. We were both breathing hard, gasping for air when he held me away from him.

"Time to get up, we'll continue this later."

"But I'm the birthday boy, don't I get a say in what we do today?"

Jake rolled me onto my back, gave me a quick peck on the lips and scampered from the bed before I could start something he couldn't stop.

"Spoilsport," I grumbled.

"That's me."

I watched the rise and fall of his gorgeous ass as he hurried to the bathroom. I sighed with what could have been, even though we'd fucked well into the night. It seemed I couldn't get enough of this man.

"Are you coming?" Jake shouted from the bathroom.

Since I'd moved in two weeks ago, we'd made a habit of showering together. A very nice habit I might add.

I rolled my aching body from the bed and headed for the bathroom. I found Jake bent over the sink, his ass lifted in the air with a blue bow stuck on it – the type you stick on a specially wrapped gift. A bottle of lube was on the benchtop beside him. My dick which had started to soften, instantly hardened.

In the four months we'd been together, Jake had never bottomed and I hadn't asked him to. I figured it was something he didn't like to do and I loved having him inside me so it didn't matter. I stepped closer, my eyes on his as he watched me in the mirror.

"Jake?"

"Happy Birthday, Gorgeous. Come and open your present."

"Really? You'll bottom? I thought you didn't like to."

"I've only bottomed once and it hurt like hell so I refused to do it again. It was because I wasn't prepped. I want this. I want you to know how I feel when I'm inside you. I want to feel you deep inside me."

I moved closer, removed the bow and dropped it into the sink. Jake turned his head and we kissed gently.

"Thank you, but you don't have to do this."

"I want to, Honey. Just take it slow."

"Slow it is."

I kneeled behind Jake and spread his cheeks. His rosy, puckered hole fluttered in anticipation. I grazed my thumb across it and Jake moaned. He spread his legs wider and I crawled between them. My mouth watered and I licked my suddenly dry lips before lowering my head and exploring his hole with my tongue. The taste was musky, not unpleasant.

My confidence grew, I grabbed the lube and squeezed a generous amount onto three fingers. I threw it back onto the bench and slowly slid the first finger inside. Jake flinched and his hole tensed. I rubbed the other hand over his ass cheek in a soothing motion.

"Relax, Babe. I won't hurt you."

I'd never done this before but I'd taken note of how Jake had always prepared me. Jake slowly relaxed. I slid the finger through his tight ring of muscle and paused while he adjusted. When he pushed back against me, I eased in deeper. He dropped his head onto his arms.

"Are you okay?"

"It feels fucking amazing."

I kissed the small of his back and added a second finger. The muscle collapsed and the third finger slid in with no resistance. I stretched and widened Jake's hole while I searched for his gland. I knew from experience how incredible the slightest brush of the prostate felt. When I managed to find it and push my middle finger against the spongy bundle, Jake almost shot through the ceiling. His ass clenched and I took the opportunity to brush against it again.

"Fuck, all this time I had no idea. Now, I understand your reaction."

"It feels good, huh?"

"It feels fucking amazing. I need you, Lee."

I glanced around.

"Condom?"

"I don't want you to use one. Our tests were both clear and I want to feel you inside me without a barrier."

I lathered my dick with lube and lined the head up at his entrance. I was trembling, I'd never been inside a man before. Slowly I pushed forward and felt the ring of muscle soften completely and give way. Once I'd penetrated I held still so Jake could adjust. His head was still resting on his arms and I couldn't see what he was feeling.

"Lift your head, Babe. Look at us in the mirror. Watch how we make each other feel."

Jake snapped his eyes to mine in the mirror, they blazed with lust.

I watched his face carefully while I pushed deeper. I was long and thick, well-endowed, Jake said on more than one occasion. I didn't want to hurt him like he'd been hurt before. I wanted him to enjoy my birthday present.

Inch by delectable inch, I sought out the depths. He was warm and his channel squeezed me hard. It felt fucking amazing. When my balls sat against his and I was as deep as I could go, I wrapped an arm around his chest and nipped at his ear before licking it soothingly.

"How do you feel?" I asked his image in the mirror.

"Full. Incredible. You're perfect."

Jake pushed back against me. I dropped my hand to his cock, wrapped around it and tugged. Pre-cum dripped to the floor.

"Fuck me, Lee."

I pulled back. Pushed inside. Twisted my hips and hit his prostate which caused him to let loose with a string of expletives.

"Harder. Faster," he demanded.

I increased the pace, hitting him hard. Jake's cock swelled in my hand. He started to drop his head back onto his hands. I lifted my hand from his hip and wrenched his head back by using a fistful of hair. His eyes were glazed over. Wrapping an arm around his chest, I pulled him into me closer and hammered his ass.

"Look in the mirror, Jake. Look at how gorgeous you are."

Our eyes met seconds before his ass clenched and his dick shot cum all over my hand.

"Oh my g...g........fuck......LEE!"

The gripping of his ass on my cock pushed me over the edge. I screamed his name and flooded his insides. Black spots peppered my eyes with the force of the ejaculation. When we were finally released from the grip of our orgasms, I slumped against Jake's back. We were both swimming in sweat and puffing loudly. When Jake stood, I slid out and cum trickled down his legs. When he turned to stare at me, my heart skipped a beat.

Realization hit with the force of a sledgehammer.

Somehow.

Somewhere along the line.

I'd fallen in love with this man.

***

"Ready to go?" Jake asked as he picked up his keys from the kitchen bench.

"Do we have to go?"

"Yes. Mama and the guys will be disappointed if we don't turn up. She's closed the restaurant until six tonight so you could have your birthday lunch there without being disturbed. And, Roan and I closed the club for the night."

"I know, it's just I can think of much better things we could be doing."

"We'll have all night to do whatever you can think of."

Jake brushed his lips over mine, gathered my hand and led me from the apartment. The days were becoming cooler and I turned the collar of my jacket up as we pushed into the wind and walked briskly toward the restaurant.

Jake held the door open for me to enter and a roar of Happy Birthday greeted me. Mama waddled over, faster than I'd ever seen her move and pulled me into her arms. The air left my lungs with an audible "oomph."

"Buon compleanno, bel ragazzo."

"Mama." Jake gave Mama a faux scowl.

"Happy Birthday, beautiful boy," she corrected. "Come, sit down. You have guest of honor seat and your man shall be on one side, Mama will be on the other. I have all your favorite dishes."

I kissed Mama's cheek and she led me to the center of a long table she'd set up with the help of her staff. I wanted to shake hands with the other men and thank them for coming but she was having none of it.

The table was decorated with crackers and balloons with the number eighteen sprayed on them, floated in the air. Streamers hung from the walls, penis candies were scattered about on the table and drinking straws were also in the shape of a penis. Mama never failed to surprise us with her liberal mind.

Jake pulled out a chair and I was seated in front of a mountain of gifts. I blushed with embarrassment and turned to face Jake when he sat beside me.

"These are all for me?"

"I'm not aware of anyone else's birthday, are you?"

"Jake," I whispered, tears thick in my eyes. "It's too much."

Jake leaned over, pulled me against his chest and kissed me. "These are your friends, sweetheart. We all love you. You mean a lot to us."

In the months since I'd attempted suicide, these men and Mama had rallied around me to ensure it wouldn't happen again. In the beginning, they'd had no idea what was behind the attempt and not one of them had asked. Over time, I'd sat down with each of them and explained about my past. Not one of them judged me. Every one of them had said the same as Jake – I was a teenager who hadn't thought things through and considered the consequences. Each man had spoken about the mistakes in their own pasts and how if it hadn't been for Roan and Jake, they'd probably be dead on a street corner somewhere. They convinced me, I wasn't as bad as I'd believed. Despite feeling much better, I was still nowhere near asking my family for the forgiveness I craved. I was still fragile and was afraid their rejection would push me back onto the ledge.

When I eventually decided to ask be a part of their lives again, I knew Jake would be by my side giving me strength. For now, I had Jake, the rest of the men, Mama and Jake's parents, who I was quickly coming to love.

I straightened in my seat and smiled at the sea of faces which were watching me. "Let's get this party started!"

Everyone cheered, hooted and hollered. I stood and one by one, they came to me, kissed my cheek and shook my hand.

Jake's mother pulled me into a bear hug and smothered my face with kisses. His father shook my hand and hugged me tight. When everyone had returned to their seats, I sat and began opening gifts. To say I'd been spoiled was an understatement.

By the time I was done, I had three new cashmere sweaters in various colors, a gorgeous wool coat in navy blue, two wool caps, CDs of various artists and Pedro – who I quickly learned was the clown of the group, had given me a dozen G-strings for use at home. Each pair had a downright crude saying on the front.

Jake's Mom and Dad moved the gifts onto a table off to one side and Mama's waiters and waitresses began serving the meals. As usual, the food was delicious and there was plenty of it. I didn't think I could eat another bite when Mama came from the kitchen, a cake in her hands. A number eighteen candle blazed, flanked by two spitting sparklers. I licked my lips when she approached – she'd made me a Tiramisu cake, my absolute favorite thing to eat.

I waited for everyone to sing Happy Birthday and blew out the candle to loud applause. Mama then dished up the cake, the first piece to me. I moaned as I took the first mouthful and when I turned to Jake, his eyes were burning with lust.

I forked a piece into his mouth before kissing him. The cake moved back and forth in our mouths as our tongues tangled. It was decadent, bordering on erotic. When we moved apart, Jake brushed the corner of my mouth with his finger before he pushed the piece of cake between my lips and kissed me gently.

The afternoon was filled with good food, wine and beer for all except me, laughter and talking. It was almost four when Jake said we needed to make a move so Mama and her staff would have enough time to clean up the place. His parents offered to drop off my gifts as they had their car and there was too much for us to carry.

"Before everyone leaves, I'd like to give Lee the gift I have for him."

My head snapped around to Jake, he'd already given me the wool coat. I couldn't imagine what else he might have for me. He reached into his pocket and pulled out a blue velvet box. My hand shook as I accepted it from him.

"Happy Birthday, Sweetheart."

"Thank you but you didn't have to."

"Open it."

I opened the lid and gasped. On a bed of satin lay a solid gold necklace.

"Turn it over."

I did. "One the back, in tiny engraved letters it read – *Wherever you are, my heart will be with you. Jake.*

Tears sprang to my eyes and I threw myself into his arms. "It's gorgeous, I love it."

After kissing deeply, he fastened it around my neck. I swore I would always have it with me.

After thanking everyone and more kissing and hugging, Jake and I said our goodbyes and headed home.

It had been one of the best days of my life.

The best day had been when I'd met Jake.

# Chapter Twenty

**JAKE**

*Liam's First Show*

I woke with the mother of all headaches and after extracting myself from Liam who was wrapped around me like a candy wrapper, I slid from the bed. I pulled on a pair of sweats and padded to the kitchen. A box of painkillers the doctor had given me sat on the bench. I grabbed a glass, filled it with water and swallowed two of the blue pills down. I hated poisoning my body with chemicals but for the past few months, the headaches had become steadily worse. I resolved to re-visit the doctor, maybe some kind of test might show what was really going on.

I didn't want to disturb Lee, it was his first show tonight and I knew he hadn't been sleeping well due to nerves. There was no doubt in my mind he'd be a huge success. Watching the final dress rehearsal yesterday, I'd stood riveted to the spot as he'd leapt, twisted and turned. He was a natural and I had no doubt, once word got out the club would be packed on the nights that he danced.

I stood staring out over the harbor below. Dawn hadn't as yet heralded a new day. It was still dark out and reflected lights from buildings and moored boats danced on the water's surface. I hadn't heard Liam move up behind me. His arms wrapped around my waist and I leaned back into his embrace. He gently kissed my cheek.

"Another headache?"

"They're getting worse. I'll make an appointment to see the doctor tomorrow."

Lee spun me around to face him, the movement caused me to become giddy and I stumbled.

"Come and sit down." He led me to the sofa and eased me down before he sat beside me and pulled me into his arms. "I'll come with you. I want answers. I'm worried about you."

"I'm sure it's nothing. The doctor said it was underlying stress and worry. Probably just anxious about your first show."

Lee shook his head. "I'm not so sure. Make the appointment...... For me?"

"How could I refuse you? The pain has dulled, let's go back to bed." I winced with pain as I stood and Liam frowned. "I'm fine, Honey. I don't want you worrying about me, focus on your show. You're gonna knock 'em dead."

We climbed into bed and Liam drew me into his arms before kissing the top of my aching head. I wriggled closer and it wasn't long before I heard his breathing even out – he was asleep.

*\*\**

Every employee of the club had turned up to support Lee on his first night. The place was packed and for the first time ever, women had come to watch. Word about a new dancer had spread like wildfire throughout town. Knowing this, caused Lee to be as nervous as hell. He'd stood trembling in my arms, terrified he'd let us all down. After reassuring him, he'd be perfect, Pedro had taken him downstairs to get ready. Lee was on first at eight o'clock, Sam would follow. At eleven, Dixon was the lead dancer and Lee was after him.

I made my way over to the bar where Roan and Joey were perched on stools watching the room. Trace and Jenkins were busy with customers. Music blared from speakers, in time with the throbbing in my skull. I stood beside my brother and dragged a hand over my head.

"Nervous?" Roan asked.

"Yeah. I'll be glad when his first dance is done, it should help settle the nerves in both of us."

Roan studied me closely.

"You look like shit. Your eyes are bloodshot and they're dark like someone has thumped you. Are you okay?"

"Headaches are getting worse. I'm seeing the doctor tomorrow morning."

"Tell him you want them investigated. You've been having them regularly for months and I'd never known you to have a damn thing wrong with you before they started."

I squeezed at the back of my neck, hoping to ease the vise like pain.

"I will."

The music in the club quieted. Lights dimmed. The stage lights turned off completely. My stomach performed somersaults. Roan's voice boomed out over the speakers in a pre-recorded announcement:

*"Welcome to The Velvet Post.*

*This man will have you welcoming the Devil himself.*

*Sit back.*

*Relax.*

*Remember the rules.*

*And now, for you pleasure and enjoyment.*

*Please welcome to the stage in his debut performance – Lee!"*

Clapping, wolf whistling and hollering followed but when music blasted into the room, everyone silenced. A red spotlight beamed down onto the center of the stage. Smoke billowed and Lee, crouched over, covered with black feathered wings and holding the pole, rose from the floor.

The pole jerked into place and he slowly unfolded. The wings extended out from his back and tiny red lights began flashing. While one hand and foot remained on the pole, the others extended out to the side. His head snapped up to reveal his masked face and the crowd clapped.

The routine had the crowd mesmerized. Twists. Turns. Flips. Splits. Leaps into the air which defied gravity. The man was exquisite. The glittering red G-string had no hope of holding the money being thrust into it when he danced to the edge of the stage and swung his hips as he lowered to the people standing there. Most of the cash was thrown onto the stage.

Johnny and Balati stood guarding my man, ensuring no harm would come to him. The routine appeared to go off without a hitch and by the time Lee was lowered beneath the floor, out of sight, the crowd was going wild.

Roan shook my hand and clapped me on the back.

"You did well, little brother. I've never seen anyone like him. He's as close to perfection as you can get when it comes to dance. Go and tell him – well done."

Joey, Trace and Jenkins seconded Roan's words. I threaded my way through the crowd and headed for the stairs leading down to the dressing room. Johnny stood guard so no-one could slip down to the dancers.

"He did good, Boss."

"He certainly did."

I jogged down the steps and heard the excited chatter before I reached the dressing room. When I stepped into the doorway, Lee was surrounded by the other men who were hugging him, shaking his hand and clapping him on the back. He'd removed the wings and mask and stood wearing only the G-string. He was stunningly beautiful.

When I stepped into the room and Lee saw me, his face lit up. He raced toward me and jumped into my arms, his legs wrapped around my waist. I held him close and peppered his face with kisses.

"You were amazing, Honey. I'm so proud of you. Roan, Joey, Trace and Jenkins were impressed."

"It felt good, Jake. Almost like I belonged up there. I didn't stuff up and let you down."

I hugged him tight. "You could never let me down. Do you want to get changed and come up to the office? I ordered in sandwiches, they'll be light on your stomach."

"I'll take a quick shower and come up." He took my face in his hands. "You look terrible."

"I'm fine. Go and take that shower and come upstairs."

I kissed him thoroughly before he lowered his feet back to the floor.

"I'm hitting the shower and going upstairs guys."

The other dancers waved their hands or nodded and I walked Lee to the shower block.

"Don't be long." I gave his bare ass a squeeze before turning to head back upstairs.

*** 

Lee's first night had gone without a hitch. He'd been a smash hit as I'd known he would be. The man came to life up on stage and I'd never been prouder of him. We'd celebrated his success by exploring every inch of each other well into the small hours of the morning.

On waking, my head had been pounding again or more accurately – still. I needed answers, I couldn't continue feeling the way I was.

I held Lee close to my side as we headed down the street to Doctor Vaughan's office. We were both rugged up in coats, gloves and hats. The weather had turned chilly and the wind, which slapped at my face felt like it was full of ice.

When we reached the office, I held the door open and we both slipped inside quickly. The space was warm and as I approached the receptionist, I shrugged off my coat before removing the gloves and hat. Lee did the same. The woman asked us to have a seat and I held Lee's hand as we sat waiting.

Ten minutes later, a nurse called me through. She smiled at Lee as we joined her. We followed her down a hallway and into a room where the doctor sat behind a desk. He swiveled his chair to face us as we entered. I sat in a chair nearest to him. Lee sat beside me, clutching my hand.

"This is Lee, my boyfriend," I said to the doctor.

He smiled and shook Lee's hand. "Pleased to meet you. You're new to town?"

"Yes. I've only been here just over five months."

"All of us from the club see Doctor Vaughan when needed," I explained.

"Right, let's get down to business. What's been happening?"

"The headaches are getting worse. Sometimes they're so bad I can barely keep my eyes open. The pain causes vomiting and dizziness. I'm worried there's something other than stress causing them."

The doctor nodded and scribbled in a file before standing over me. He shone a light into my eyes and had me looking this way and that. He sat down and scribbled some more. I have no idea how he knew what he'd written, his handwriting was a mess. He placed the pen down and turned to me.

"You look like shit, are you sleeping?"

I should explain. Doctor Vaughan says it like it is. He's not one for bedside manners which is why I've stuck with him for the past five and a half years.

Lee spoke before I could answer. "Not a lot, he gets up at all hours of the night and takes pain pills but they don't seem to help. I've heard him moaning in pain and vomiting sometimes, too." I turned to Lee. I'd thought he'd been asleep when the pain had forced me from the bed. "I wake the second you move, Jake. I know you're suffering."

"I think there might be something more happening here. I'm going to send you for an urgent MRI. Have you had problems with balance? Speech? Walking?"

"I stumble now and again but speech has been fine."

The doctor printed off a request form and handed it to Jake. "Go straight up to Nollett Imaging and get this done. I'll call them and let them know you're on your way. I should have the results later this afternoon and I'll be in touch."

"What do you think it is, Doctor?" Lee's expression was one of anxiety.

"I have a couple of ideas but let's wait for the results before we start worrying."

His words didn't seem to put Lee at ease, he was trembling slightly. I stood and pulled Lee onto his feet before shaking hands with the doctor.

"Thanks, I'll wait to hear from you."

We left the office, donned our winter clothing and stepped back into the frigid cold. Lee was squeezing the blood from my hand, I could feel his fear. I stopped and turned him toward me.

"Calm down, Honey. I'm sure if it was really bad he'd have sent us to the hospital."

Lee smiled but I didn't miss the tears in his eyes. I drew him close for a hug, kissed his cold cheek and we hurried up to the Imaging center.

*** 

Lee was at my desk entering the figures from the previous day, it was his day off from the books as he was dancing but he'd insisted it would take his mind off what was happening with me. I'd been talking with Trace when the call from the doctor came – it was just after lunch. Lee was pale, ghostlike as he rushed toward me. I pulled him into my arms when he reached me, I'd never seen him so upset.

"What's wrong?"

"Doctor Vaughan called, he wants to see you now. He said he doesn't care what you're doing, you have to get down there." Tears flowed from my man's fear filled eyes.

"Calm down, Sweetheart. Everything will be fine, I'm sure." Despite my words, I was terrified of what the tests must have found.

We dressed back in our winter layers and hurried down to the doctor's office. The nurse led us straight through. Doctor Vaughan was at his desk and turned to face us, a deep frown marred his face.

"Sit down."

Lee shook life a leaf on a breeze. I wasn't a whole lot better.

"The radiologist sent through your images." He spun the computer screen to face us. A black and white picture filled the screen. The doctor picked up his pen and indicated a large, round area that was at the bottom and slightly off center. "This is your brain, Jake. The large white area is a tumor."

*A fucking tumor? I was gonna die?*

"No," Lee whimpered before burying his head into my chest.

The doctor patted Lee's back. "Calm down. It's large, about the size of a golf ball and is called a Meningioma. More than likely the tumor is benign and it appears to have been there for quite a while, maybe even years. They can be very slow growing and symptoms don't become apparent until they press on nerves. I've made an appointment for you to see Doctor Scales at County at four this afternoon. He's a Neurosurgeon. He'll remove the tumor which should see the end of the headaches."

"Is it urgent that I have it removed?"

"Not life-threatening urgent but if it's left, it may cause seizures which could have long lasting effects on brain function. As the headaches are becoming more severe, I believe seizures are a very real possibility."

He handed me an envelope with Dr. Scales name written on the front and the address of where his rooms were located within County Hospital. We all stood.

"Dr. Scales will answer any questions you have. He's a good doctor, you can trust him."

"Thank you." I felt like I'd dropped into an alternate universe. Brain tumor? How could this be happening?

Lee helped me into my coat, I was in a daze. Not exactly frightened, the doctor's words had been reassuring. I was.....I don't know what I was. Stunned? Relieved that I knew the cause of the debilitating pain? Worried about something going wrong? Fuck, how was I going to break the news to Mom? She would be hysterical when she found out. Roan could explain it to her, he was the eldest. My big brother. They were supposed to handle everything, weren't they?

We trudged up to a coffee shop close to County. I didn't want to face the men at the club. Once we were seated at a table, our coats, hats and gloves off once again, I pulled out my phone and called Roan.

Lee gripped my hand as I explained what we'd been told. Roan let flow a string of expletives before making me promise I'd keep him informed. He ordered - regardless of when the surgery took place - I wasn't to return to the club until it was done and I'd recovered. I had no problem with leaving it in his and Joey's hands but I hated not being there for Lee.

I disconnected the call and shoved the phone into my pocket.

"How did he take it?" Lee asked.

"Not great, he's my big brother and he's worried. He's going to drive out and tell Dad. Dad can then tell Mom. She won't take it well, everything gets blown way out of proportion with her. I remember, when I was about seven or eight, I fell off my bike and took the skin off my knuckles. Mom rushed me to the doctor and insisted he do scans and tests to make sure I wouldn't get an infection from the gravel, that germs weren't burrowing into my bones."

Lee chuckled. "Did they do the tests?"

"Yep. Mom said she was paying for the fucking tests and she could ask for whatever she wanted. I think they figured it was easier to do them than to argue with her."

Lee sipped at his hot chocolate before locking his eyes with mine. "I'm scared. What if...."

I pressed my fingers gently to his mouth. "No, what ifs. Everything will be fine."

Lee nodded and we talked about how well the previous night had gone as we finished our hot drinks.

# Chapter Twenty-One

**LIAM**

I felt as if I'd been swept into the eye of a tornado. Roan had been waiting, shuffling nervously, when we arrived to meet with Doctor Scales. He hugged his brother tight and warned him, he had to be fine. Jake had told him not to be so melodramatic. That he was acting like their mother.

The doctor covered the risks of surgery, recovery time and everything else that was relevant. I didn't remember a word the doctor spoke after advising us that Jake would be having surgery first thing the following morning. He was to stay overnight so they could get him ready. I sat in stunned silence while Jake and Roan asked a plethora of questions. I have no idea how long we were in the consulting room. After what seemed like hours, Jake pulled me to my feet and we left the office.

"Where to now?" I asked.

"I have to go to admissions to get paperwork done." Jake looked at me curiously. "Weren't you listening?"

"No. Once he mentioned surgery tomorrow, I zoned out. Sorry."

Jake hugged me to his side.

"I'll cancel your shows for tonight and tomorrow so you can stay with Jake," Roan offered.

I stopped mid-stride and the men halted beside me. "No. I want to go on. I know how vicious talk can be when people don't get what they're expecting. I'll come to the hospital before and after my performances."

"Are you sure?" Roan asked.

I turned to Jake. "Do you mind?"

"Of course not. As much as I want you with me every second, there's nothing you can do and you're right – people will talk if you don't deliver."

I moved into Jake's arms and kissed him tenderly. "I need to go, I'm late already and the boss will be pissed. I'll see you later tonight."

Jake lowered his lips to mine and kissed me with so much passion, I wanted to find the nearest bed and fuck him senseless. When the kiss ended, he lowered his forehead to mine. "I'll miss you."

"Only a few hours, Babe."

I reluctantly pushed from his arms.

"I'll let the others know what's happening. See you soon."

I headed toward the exit doors, turned and waved before stepping out into the cold.

*\*\*\**

"Lee, where have you been?" Pedro asked when I entered the dressing room.

"Hospital with Jake."

Pedro, Chris, Edyn and Sam all stood. They were the dancers performing tonight. Pedro and Chris after me in the eight thirty slot, Edyn and Sam before me at eleven. The others performed in both duos and as solo performers. Tonight, were both duos.

"Why the fuck were you at the hospital?" Chris demanded to know.

I explained everything that had happened throughout the day. The men paled as I spoke. They had known Jake for a long time and it was obvious they adored him.

"Fuck." - Pedro.

"Shit." - Edyn.

"He'll come through this," Chris assured and I prayed he was right.

"I'm going to go upstairs and let the other men know. I'll be back down shortly."

Trace and Jenkins worked the bar. Johnny and Balati were both working as was usual for a Friday night. Roan had called Joey and he hadn't hesitated to come in. Clint, Mason, Neil, Alex and Paul were also in along with the newest waiter - Oliver. I managed to bring each of them up to date and various expletives were spoken on hearing about Jake.

Returning downstairs, I dropped into a chair and texted Tommy and Dixon the news about Jake. I received messages back which threatened me with bodily harm if I didn't keep in touch. I began getting ready for my performance. As worried as I was about Jake, I was determined to do my very best for him.

The club was again packed and it was standing room only. I'd made over three thousand dollars the previous night and it appeared tonight could net me close to the same.

The Devil routine went off without a hitch. I arched my back as the hot water rolled over my muscles, relaxing and soothing. I'd compromised with Tommy over time – hot shower first and then cold. He wasn't totally happy about it but accepted it was the best he'd get.

After I'd washed, I dried off and pulled on a pair of sweats and a T-shirt before heading upstairs to the office. The room was empty when I stepped inside. I pulled the door shut and moved to sit behind the desk. I hoped by working on the books it would distract me from thinking and worrying about Jake. I couldn't wait to get back to him.

Time passed quickly and before I knew it, it was time to get ready and go back on stage. It was the Angel routine this time. I wore a sparkly silver G-string, the wings were white with blue flashing lights, the mask and knee-length boots were also white. It had taken me a long time to learn how to grip the pole wearing boots but they were actually paper thin and more like a pair of stockings than real boots. A good coating of hair spray made them sticky and less prone to slipping.

This routine didn't have as many leaps and aerials as the Devil routine but did have more spins and tricks on the pole itself. I found them both equally challenging and even though the patrons seemed to prefer the Devil routine, I had a soft spot for the Angel.

I nailed every part of the routine and when I slid beneath the floor, I jumped down and hurried to the dressing room. I stripped, showered and dressed in record time. Within thirty minutes, I was at the door to Jake's room. Roan had texted me the information earlier.

\*\*\*

When I pushed through the door I found Roan slumped in a chair by the wall. The bed was gone! I looked around frantically for any sign of Jake. My heart thumped in my chest. Roan's eyes were red rimmed. As I moved toward him, he stood. I walked into his open arms and he held me close.

"Where is he?"

"Surgery."

A lump lodged in my throat, I was almost too afraid to ask.

"Why?"

"About seven o'clock we were sitting here talking. He complained his head felt like it was going to explode. He slumped in the bed and started thrashing uncontrollably. His eyes were rolled back in his head and he was foaming at the mouth."

"Seizure?"

"Yeah, a bad one. I shouted for a nurse. He called for help and asked me to leave the room. Next thing I knew, Dr. Scales was here and said theater was free and he was doing the surgery immediately. They wheeled Jake out about fifteen minutes later. He was out cold but settled. I was terrified, Lee."

"Have you called your parents?"

"I called Dad and told him what had happened. He didn't want Mom causing problems here so I'm going to call him when Jake is out of surgery. He'll bring her in then. I'm sorry I didn't call you but I knew you'd only worry and there was nothing you could do."

"That's fine. I would have rushed down here and worried myself into a panic. Hopefully, we won't have to wait too long for him to be brought back in."

"We can go upstairs to the recovery waiting room now you're here. They'll take him there from surgery and we can see him."

We left the room and dashed for the elevators. Recovery was on the fifth floor and we were currently on the third. Roan pushed the button and we stepped inside when the doors opened. As the elevator moved upward, we stood in silence. As soon as the doors opened, we followed the signs to the waiting room.

"Did Dr. Scales say how long surgery would take?"

"Between four to six hours so he could be out any time now."

Roan had just finished speaking when Dr. Scales pushed through two large doors and approached us. He had a smile on his face and I sighed with relief.

"He's doing great, the tumor has been completely removed. I expect he will recover completely despite the seizure. I'll keep him here for around five days and then he can go home. He'll need to take things easy for about a month. I'll see him in ten days in my rooms. He should be out in a few minutes and you'll be able to see him."

I shook hands with the doctor and felt tears pricking my eyes. To say I was grateful, relieved was an understatement. Roan also thanked him before moving away to call their parents.

Ten minutes later a nurse came to find us. She explained Jake was awake but drowsy and we'd be able to see him. It took everything in me to follow her quietly instead of charging into the room and scooping Jake into my arms. I saw him straight away. His eyes were closed and the lines of pain in his face, which had previously had me so worried, were gone.

Roan and I approached the bed quietly, not wanting to disturb him from his sleep. He must have sensed we were there, his bruised eyes flickered open and he lifted his hand to me. I slid my palm into his, leaned over and kissed his cheek. Thick white bandages blanketed his head. Roan slid a chair behind where I stood and I sat. He pulled up another and sat beside me.

"How are you feeling, little brother?"

"Like a truck ran over my head."

Jake's speech was slightly slurred but we'd been told to expect it.

"You should feel better in the next few days, Babe. Then, I can take you home and spoil you."

"How did dance go?"

"Great. The place was packed again. The guys all send their love and said they'll work out a visitor schedule so they don't overwhelm you or the hospital."

"Probably a good idea.' Jake looked to his brother. "Mom and Dad?"

"I've kept Dad updated. He didn't tell Mom you'd gone into surgery, you know how she is."

Jake nodded and winced.

"They're on their way here. I expect Dad will cop an earful for not telling Mom."

"He'll be relegated to the spare room for a while."

Jake's eyes drifted shut and he slept.

"I'll go and wait for Mom and Dad."

I nodded as he left and lowered my forehead to where I held tightly to Jake's hand. I was well aware things could still go wrong but I convinced myself it was over and my man would be back to normal in no time.

***

It was just after midnight when Jake's mom and dad – Janet and Harvey, rushed in. I moved aside so Janet could gather her son in her arms. Her face was tear streaked, her eyes, red. She looked as upset as I felt.

"Mom, don't over-react." Jake spoke quietly, his voice hoarse.

"You're my beautiful baby boy, I'll overreact if I want to. I was so scared when your father told me what had happened. He's sleeping in the guest room for a month and I'm still deciding about how to punish Roan."

Harvey moved to the other side of the bed, bent over and kissed his son's forehead. "It's good to see you came through okay, son."

"Thanks, Dad."

"Your brother said you've been having headaches for months, why didn't you say something?" Janet held Jake's hand with one of hers and stroked it with the other.

"They weren't bad at first. When they got worse, I saw the doctor. He thought it was stress. I knew you'd start demanding tests and I didn't think there was a need for them. I'm a big boy, Mom, I can look after my own health now."

"You're my baby boy and I need to look after you. You can come home when you leave here and I'll take care of you."

Jake cut his heavy eyes to me. "No, Mom. I'm going home with Lee."

Janet spun around and placed a hand on my arm. "Lee, oh darling, I totally forgot about you. I've been so used to Jake being on his own. I'm so sorry. You must have been frantic with worry."

"I was scared to death." I moved around her and gathered Jake's hand. "I love your son very much, I don't know what I would have done if something had happened."

"Y..y..you love me?" Jake asked softly.

I leaned forward and kissed his lips. "I love you, Jake."

A tear slid from one eye. "I love you too, Lee."

I kissed him again and when I stood and turned toward his mom, I saw the tears in her eyes. She pulled me into her arms and kissed my cheek. At that moment in time, I found myself missing my own mom more than ever.

"Now you're all here, I'm going to head home. I'll be back in the morning, Jake." Roan patted Jake's arm, kissed his mother's cheek and nodded at both me and his father.

"Thanks, Roan...for everything."

"Any time, little brother."

When Roan left the room, the rest of us sat. Jake drifted back off to sleep. It was going to be a long few days until I could take my love home.

# Chapter Twenty-Two

**LIAM**

The next few days passed without incident. I'd been at the hospital with Jake at every possible opportunity, returning to the club only to perform or hurriedly make entries into the books. I'd told Roan to reduce my pay since I wasn't working my full number of hours but he refused to even consider it. He'd argued I was taking care of one of the clubs most important assets – one of the owners. Jake had been stoked with how well my first nights on stage had gone. I'd made almost eight thousand dollars! He'd healed well. There'd been no sign of any more headaches and scans had shown everything was healing well inside. He was free to return home. The nurse sat him in a wheelchair, citing it was hospital policy until he was out of the building. Jake hadn't protested too badly, he was too eager to go home.

\*\*\*

We held hands as the elevator rose to our floor. I unlocked the door to our apartment and led Jake inside. He was still pale and I'd been warned it would be a couple of weeks before he was feeling like his old self.

"Do you want to go to bed or relax on the sofa?" I dropped the keys on the table by the door.

Jake gave me a mischievous smile. "Bed, if you're coming too."

I shook my head. "Nah ah, doc said nothing strenuous for a couple of weeks."

"I can't wait a couple of weeks, I want you now."

I stepped closer and folded him into my arms before pressing a kiss to his lips. My hand roamed over the bald patch on his head which was now covered with prickly stubble where his hair had begun to grow back. I felt the coarseness of stitches which wouldn't be removed for another week. It was a reminder of what he'd been through. When he attempted to get handsy and take things further than a kiss, I pushed away and guided him to sit down. I placed a pillow at one end for his head and lifted his legs onto the soft cushion so he was lying down. When I started to move away, Jake grabbed my hand.

"Sit with me, you look exhausted."

Jake spread his legs and I climbed between them to lie on my side over his body. I rested my head against his chest and sighed. It felt 'normal' again.

"Did you mean it?" Jake asked.

I lifted my head to gaze up at him. "Mean what?"

"What you said when you saw me after surgery."

"Yes. I love you, Jake. I was terrified when I thought I might lose you. You've become everything to me."

Jake hugged me close and kissed the top of my head. "I love you, too. I tried so hard to stay away when you first arrived in town. I thought I was too old for you, that you'd never be interested in me. I'm glad I listened to my heart instead of my head."

"Not as glad as I am." I yawned and lowered my head.

"Get some sleep, beautiful."

The last thing I remembered was Jake's kiss on my hair before drifting into the blessed darkness of sleep.

\*\*\*

*Three Years Later*

**JAKE**

I sat beside Roan at the bar and watched as Lee descended back below stage. As usual, his performance had been flawless. My man was poetry in motion and I could never get enough of his dancing. More importantly, I couldn't get enough of him – both his body and mind. He'd matured into a wonderful human being and the other men adored him. Even though he was a star, he never once allowed it to affect him. He always considered others before himself.

Roan and I had been approached numerous time by film directors, producers and agents – all wanting a piece of Lee. We'd sat him down and explained, if he took any of their offers, he could be a superstar on the world stage. I didn't want him to accept any of the carrots they dangled before him, but it had to be Lee's decision. If it was what he wanted, I'd be right there beside him, giving him the support he needed. But, he refused. He wouldn't even entertain the idea of dancing elsewhere, being involved in film or in stage shows. He insisted, he was happy where he was and had no intention of leaving. I worried he felt obligated to us but he flatly denied it.

I pushed off the stool and headed toward my office. Lee would shower and change and spend the time between shows with me. We'd have something to eat and while he entered figures into the books, I'd usually sit on the sofa and read, sneaking glances now and again. There was no doubt in my mind that I was deeply in love with my man. I often wondered how I'd ever lived without him.

I paused at the office door to take one last look back into the main area of the club. Sam was on stage and the crowd stood riveted. It was Friday night, the second busiest of the week. The place was jammed full. Either Johnny or Balati were required to guard the entrance doors these days, to monitor the number of people entering. On the three nights Lee performed, people were turned away in droves. Despite us having approval for two hundred patrons at any one time.

As usual, the crowd was a balanced mix of men and women. As I stepped forward to enter the office, a man approached. He was tall with dark hair and the most brilliant blue eyes I'd ever seen. He appeared to be headed for the steps which led down to the dressing room. I placed a hand on his chest as he reached me, bringing him to a stop.

"Whoa, there. No-one is allowed downstairs."

The man stepped back and dragged his hand over his head. "I have to speak with my brother. Please, it's taken me over three years to find him. "

"Brother?"

"Liam Masters."

Realization dawned. "You're Steve."

"You know about me?"

"Yes, Lee talks about you now and again." I pulled the door to the office closed, grabbed Steve's arm and attempted to lead him across the floor to the stock room.

Steve pulled back and wrenched himself free of my hand. "I'm not leaving until I speak to my brother."

"Steve, I'm Jake. I own this club and I've been your brother's partner for over three years. Please, come with me. I have an idea."

He nodded and followed me willingly. Mason was serving a table and I tapped his shoulder.

"Keep an eye out for Lee and tell him I'll be there shortly. I'm just with a client."

Mason nodded and Steve and I continued on our way. Once in the stockroom, I closed and locked the door.

"Sorry, but I don't want Lee to know you're here."

Steve began to protest but I held up a hand.

"Hear me out. Sunday is Lee's twenty-first birthday and we have a party planned at Mama's. I'd like you and your family to be there."

I gave Steve the details of Mama's and he entered the address into his phone.

"The restaurant will be closed for our function. What did you think of Lee?"

"He's amazing. I didn't know he was so talented."

"There are probably a lot of things about him you don't know. Do you think your parents would like to come and see him dance tomorrow night? You'll need to stay toward the back of the club and out of sight, I don't want him seeing any of you until Sunday."

"I'll ask. Can we meet for coffee somewhere tomorrow, I'd like to talk with you?"

"Of course. There's a French café called *Le Petit* on Cross Street. Lee leaves for the club at ten so how about ten thirty?"

"I'll see you then. Thanks, Jake."

I opened the door and led Steve out, I knew Lee wouldn't be on the floor. As agreed, he'd stayed away during opening hours while he was underage. After showing Steve to the door, I shook his hand, said goodnight and watched as he headed down the street before returning to my office.

***

Steve was seated at a table in the far corner of the café when I entered, an empty cup sat in front of him. As I approached, he stood and held out his hand which I shook before we both sat.

"Thanks for agreeing to meet with me, Jake."

A waitress approached and we both ordered coffee with a piece of carrot cake. Once she'd left, we got down to business.

"How is he? Mom gets a note from him every month but all it says is he's happy and doing well."

"He is happy....*we're* happy. I love your brother very much and he loves me. He told me about what happened and why he'd left home. He said after you found him in Linton, he knew he had to move again because you wouldn't have left him alone. I met him the day after he arrived here. He was staying in the motel across the road from the club. I offered him a job as our bookkeeper and dancer. He was reluctant to learn to dance at first. He insisted you were the one who was good at everything but promised to give it a try. You saw the result last night."

"Unfortunately, Liam grew up in my shadow and none of us realized how he was struggling until it was too late. We just thought he was spoiled and wild."

"There was a lot going on in that head of his. It hasn't been easy for him, Steve. He doesn't say but I know he misses all of you. I see it in his eyes when we visit my Mom and Dad. When he first came here, it was tough and I nearly lost him. He still has nightmares and insists none of you will ever forgive him."

"We do forgive him but he wouldn't listen when I tried to tell him." Steve pauses for a moment and frowns. "Lost him?"

"He attempted suicide for the second time."

"The second time?"

I waited for the waitress to place our order onto the table and move away before speaking again.

"The first time was not long after you visited in Linton. He didn't cut deep enough and the bleeding stopped. He didn't make that mistake the second time, but fortunately, one of the other dancers was suspicious after something Lee had said and decided to check on him. He'd slashed his wrists and was bleeding to death. If Tommy had been five minutes later, Lee wouldn't have made it."

Steve was visibly shocked and upset. "We had no idea. Why the fuck didn't someone contact us?"

"None of us knew where you were. Lee refused to tell us. I'm so sorry. I'm a trained Trauma Psychologist and with the approval of the Psychiatrist who the hospital appointed, I was able to counsel him. I tried to convince him that he was young and hadn't thought of the consequences. He can't get past the fact you and Keegan were almost killed and her baby died. I've tried so many times to get him to at least talk with you but he's refused."

"Thank you for all you've done for my brother."

"You don't need to thank me, I'd do anything for him. He's my whole life and I love him more than I ever thought it was possible to love someone. Did you speak with your parents?"

"Yes. They were over the moon when I told them I'd found him but they were concerned when I explained what he was doing. I think they'll feel better when they see for themselves. They've agreed to come tomorrow and on Sunday. Uncle Wade and Uncle Rafe will be coming too. I'll be bringing my wife and I'll bring the children to his party."

"Lee said you'd be married. To Keegan? Children?"

"Yes, Keegan and I are married and we have two children. A little girl who's three and a boy who's one on Liam's birthday."

"What are their names?"

"Natasha Elizabeth and Alexander Liam."

"You named your son after him....."

"Yes, we did. If that doesn't prove we love him, I don't know what will. We need him, Jake. We need him to be part of our lives. We all love him so much."

When I saw tears spring to Steve's eyes, they also filled mine. I was determined to reunite Lee with his family somehow. "Lee's told me a bit about you. He said you're a Social Worker."

"Yes. I'm also a Psychologist. I started out working in government services but the restrictions prevented my partner, Jeremy, and I from providing the support people needed. We branched out on our own about two years ago. Hired a space down in the 'hood and another uptown. The government pays us to take care of those who can't afford private treatment but it's not enough as I said. Being uptown, our clients are wealthy and can afford to pay us. The extra money covers anything else we need to provide for the less fortunate. We work both offices five days a week. I work uptown one week, Jeremy does the next. We'll never be rich but we live comfortably, keep the bills paid and get a lot of satisfaction from watching those we help turn their lives around."

"It sounds like what my brother and I were going to do when we graduated. While Roan was waiting for me to finish college, he continued dancing. He loved it and used the money to pay for college. I did the usual – waiting tables and serving behind a bar. Roan was treated pretty badly at the club where he worked and it finally became too much. Before we knew it, we were talking about opening our own club. Our dancers, wait staff and barmen are all men off the streets. Roan taught those who wanted to learn how to dance and I taught the others how to wait tables and serve behind the bar."

"It was an impressive establishment and you certainly drew a big crowd."

"That's your brother's doing. We were doing well before but since Lee has been the star attraction, business has exploded. Can I confide in you? I don't want you mentioning this to anyone else in the family."

"Of course."

"I'm going to ask Lee to marry me at his party on Sunday. I want to assure you, I have the means to take good care of him although he's wealthy in his own right thanks to his dancing. Apart from the club, my brother and I own two harbor front apartment blocks. He'll never want for anything."

Steve whistled. "Impressive but even if you weren't wealthy, knowing you love my brother is enough for any of us."

"Thank you." I glanced at my watch, it was time I met Lee for lunch. "I have to go but I'll meet you at the front door tonight at 7.45. Will that suit?"

"Yes. I look forward to you meeting our family."

We both stood, I paid the check despite Steve's protests and we headed outside. On the sidewalk, we shook hands. As I watched Steve walk away, I smiled. He appeared to be a nice man and I was looking forward to meeting the rest of Lee's family.

# Chapter Twenty-Three

**STEVE**

I was excited about seeing my brother dance again. I held Keegan's hand as I led our small group toward the entrance door of *The Velvet Post*. As he'd promised, Jake was outside on the sidewalk waiting for us. I strode toward him and shook hands before making all the introductions. My family all shook hands with the handsome man before me. I guessed he was closer to my age than Liam's but it really didn't matter.

We stood in a small circle so we could exchange a few pleasantries before entering into the noise of the club.

"Steve told us what you've done for our son, we're very grateful," Mom said to Jake.

"It's been a pleasure Mrs. Masters. I love your son so very much and more than anything, I want to see him reunited with his family. Mind you, he's not moving back home. He's mine now."

Everyone laughed. "Call me Blossom, Jake, and my husband – Hamish."

"Wade."

"Rafe."

"Ditto," Keegan smiled.

"Will do. Are you staying for both of Lee's shows?"

We all glanced at each other. "I thought you didn't want him to see us until tomorrow?" I asked.

"I don't and he won't. Because he's underage, he's not permitted in the main area of the club during opening hours. We usually have a meal in the office and he works on the books between shows. Have you eaten?"

"Yes, we have," I answered.

"Maybe a quiet drink while you wait then?"

"I think we will. It's not often we get out without the children," Keegan said with a smile.

"Okay, let's head in. The show starts promptly at eight and I don't want you to miss any of it. I'll show you where to stand so you have a clear view but where he won't be able to see you." Jake led us up the steps and the huge man guarding the door nodded and stepped aside.

"Johnny looks after the door and our dancers. Since Lee started dancing three years ago, we can't cope with the crowds and have to turn people away."

"Since Lee started?" Mom asked.

"You'll see. Our dancers are all exceptionally talented but your son is in a realm of his own. He's spectacular. We're very fortunate to have him and despite offers from Hollywood for films and Broadway stage shows, he's stayed with us."

"He's had offers from Hollywood?" Mom spoke like she couldn't believe what she was hearing.

"You'll see," Jake said again.

Jake led us to an area off to one side of the stage which gave a clear view to those watching while obscuring the dancer's view of them.

"I'll leave you here. Lee looks for me to be at the bar when he's up there and I don't want him to think something's different."

I thanked Jake and as he walked away, music blasted from the speakers. I stood with an arm around Keegan as we watched. My brother's body was perfection set to music. None of us uttered a word but on a couple of occasions when Liam flew through the air to grip the top of the pole, I hear Mom gasp and Keegan squeezed the blood from my hand. Hundreds of dollars were stuffed into his G-string and thrown onto the stage. As he lowered back into the floor and the crowd became quiet, I moved to stand in front of my parents and uncles. Mom and Dad both had tears in their eyes.

"Oh, Steve, I don't have words. He's beautiful and more talented than I ever dreamed any of our children could be." Mom brushed at her eyes, Dad held her close.

When I glanced toward my uncles, they were also brushing away tears.

"How about we find a table while there are some available. There's another dancer on now and the crowd will stay close to the stage." I noted one not far from where we stood and headed straight for it. As we lowered ourselves into chairs, Jake joined us.

"What did you think?" The question was directed at Mom and Dad.

"We don't have words, Jake. Our son is magnificent. He's certainly developed into a very handsome young man and I would never have imagined he had so much talent. I think I can speak for all of us when I say we're very proud of him," Dad said.

"His Devil routine is the crowd favorite but I love the Angel. He's the second dancer in the eleven o'clock show and his dance is full of emotion and grace. I know you'll all love it. For now, I need to meet him in the office. I'll look forward to spending time with you tomorrow.

Shall we say, ten-thirty? It will give you an hour to chat with Roan and my parents before I arrive with Lee."

"That's perfect. Thanks again, Jake. We look forward to getting to know you," Dad said.

Jake weaved his way back through the tables and headed for the steps where he'd stopped me the previous night. At the same time he reached a door off to the right, Liam appeared. It warmed my heart to watch them kiss and embrace. It was obvious, the two men were deeply in love.

A young man took our order for drinks and we settled back to watch the dancer who was currently on stage. He was also a beautiful dancer but didn't hold a candle to my brother. I supposed I was being a little bit biased.

We all chatted over drinks and discussed Liam's performance. Like I'd been the previous night, the others were amazed with his talent. Mom and Dad were relieved to have seen for themselves that their son appeared too be happy and safe. Time flew past and before we knew it, my brother returned to the stage.

Where the Devil routine had been full of drama and leaps to loud, thumping music, the Angel routine was full of grace and passion to a soft Beethoven tune.

I left the club with my family feeling a lightness I hadn't felt since Liam had left home. I couldn't wait for the party so we could meet more of his friends and the rest of his new family.

***

**LIAM**

Jake rolled me on top of his body and placed a hand to each side of my face before tilting it slightly and pressing his lips against mine. His tongue insisted on gaining entrance into my mouth and I wasn't going to deny it. His lips were full, soft and I adored kissing him. I felt his hard dick pushing into my belly while mine pushed against his.

"I love you," I murmured when he eased back.

"I love you, too. Happy Birthday, Honey. I can't believe you're twenty-one, where's the time gone?"

"I know, I'm almost an old man." I laughed at the look of horror on Jake's face.

"If you're old what the fuck am I? Have you forgotten I'll be thirty in a few months?"

"Oh, you're definitely ready for aged care," I laughed.

Jake flipped me onto my back and moved on top of me. The laughter on my lips died when I saw the smoldering lust in his eyes. I ran my hands over the firm cheeks of his ass and kissed between his shoulder and collarbone – a spot where I knew he was particularly sensitive. I'd gotten to know Jake's body extremely well over the past years. Parts of him, which when touched, caused him to squirm. Others that drove him crazy with want and a few which were unbearably ticklish. He was like a musical instrument and I was a maestro when it came to playing him. I ran my hands along the sides of his body causing him to shudder. When I reached to tweak the hardened nubs of his nipples, Jake grabbed my arms and forced them over my head.

"Leave them there."

I loved when Jake used his dominant voice. I left my hands resting over my head and lifted my hips, pushing my hard cock against his. I felt the pre-cum leaking from both of us as our dicks slid back and forth. Jake pierced me with what he probably thought was a serious glare but it didn't mask the need in his eyes.

"Lie still, let me spoil you."

"You always do."

"Not always. You've been known to do a bit of spoiling on pretty regular occasions."

I stayed still while Jake treated me to exquisite torture. There wasn't an inch of skin on my body which wasn't kissed, licked or nipped. I was burning up inside, ready to explode and he hadn't even touched my aching dick. I licked behind his ear and bit down on the lobe when he attempted to kiss me.

"Jake, please. Fuck me."

He lifted up, supporting his weight on his arms and gave me a devilish grin.

"Are you begging?"

"Are you making me beg on my birthday?"

"Good point."

Jake slid down my body and his mouth wrapped around my cock. At the same time, a finger slid inside me. My hips bucked and he didn't hesitate to swallow me deeper. My man was an expert at giving head and I felt an orgasm building. When a third finger entered me and he pushed hard against my prostate, I saw stars. I emptied into Jake's throat like I had so many times before. But, every time we came together, seemed to be more explosive.

I was still riding the crest when Jake slid inside me. Our hips rocked together and we both moaned. Another orgasm began building. I didn't know where the first one ended and the second began. Every nerve ending tingled. While Jake thrust his thick length into me, I raked my nails over his back. My legs wrapped around his waist, I needed him deeper.

My cock was trapped, I had no hope of getting a hand between us to help me come. Then again, the speed with which I was barreling towards a climax, I more than likely wouldn't need to touch myself. Jake pounded my ass, harder, faster until, white light flashed behind my eyes and I screamed my lover's name as I came.

A few pumps later and I felt the familiar warmth in my ass as Jake emptied inside me. He whispered my name over and over. His arms trembled from the effort of taking some of his weight but by the time we were both spent, they'd given out and he collapsed on top of me.

I stroked his silky soft hair and caressed his back as we lay quietly. I was looking forward to the party he and Roan had planned, but I could have easily spent the entire day in bed with my man. I'd started to drift off when Jake spoke.

"Come on, old man. We need to get you ready for your party."

I groaned when Jake rolled off me and gently coaxed me from the bed. I felt legless when my feet hit the ground but he steadied me with his hands on my waist. Lowering his head, he kissed me tenderly. I wanted more, so much more. It would have to wait until after the party.

***

I smiled at the sign on the door to Mama's restaurant. It read: *Closed for a special man's 21st birthday.* Jake had his arm around my waist and pulled me closer to him before kissing my temple.

"Ain't that the truth? You sure a special man."

"You're biased, Jake."

"I'm allowed to be, I love you."

He pushed the door open and I stepped inside. I felt my legs weaken when I immediately sighted my parents. Steve and Keegan both held a child who was the image of them. Uncle Wade and Uncle Rafe had pensive smiles on their faces. When the hell had my sisters gotten so big? I did quick calculations and realized – Kellie was now nineteen, Erin, fourteen. Fuck! While our friends and Jake's family were seated, my family were standing. I spun around and collided with Jake's chest, his arms wrapped around me.

"I don't know if I can do this, Jake." Tears burned my eyes.

He lowered his mouth to my ear and whispered. "They came looking for you, Sweetheart. It's been breaking their hearts not being able to see you. Please, for me, put the past to rest. You've earned the right to let go."

Tears streamed over my cheeks and when my eyes met Mom's, she was sobbing. I locked eyes with her and nodded. She crossed the space between us and threw herself into my arms. My tear drenched face was peppered with kisses. I had the air hugged out of me. She kept saying she was sorry and I didn't understand why she should be.

Dad was next. He knocked what little air had found its way back into my lungs, from me. He ran his hand over my head and kissed my forehead. He released his grip and leaned back, a hand remained at the back of my neck.

"I'm so fucking sorry, son. I should have talked to you, we should have worked things out. Instead, I let my anger push you away."

"You had every right to be angry, Dad. What I did was unforgiveable."

"No, it wasn't. For fuck sake, Liam, you're family and family can always forgive." I peered around Dad at the sound of an angry woman's voice – Keegan. She handed the little girl to Mom and Dad stepped aside as she approached me. She wrapped her arms around my biceps and looked at me closely.

"Josh would have found us with or without your help. Yes, you gave him the information but you didn't know what he was going to do."

"He told me, he was just going to take you back. He said he loved you and his life wasn't complete with you gone. I didn't mean to hurt you and Steve."

"You didn't hurt us, Liam. You gave Josh information he would have gotten one way or another. There's no doubt in my mind that eventually, Steve and I would have been found and beaten. You were a teenager who lost his way for a little while. You can't keep blaming yourself. Please. For me. For Steve. For your niece and nephew. Please, I'm begging you to forgive yourself."

Keegan drew me into her arms and we both cried a river of tears. After a moment or two, Steve drew her into his arms while Jake folded me into his. I was startled when Mama clapped her hands and announced enough tears had been shed and it was time to get the party started.

Music floated from the speakers, soft, enabling everyone to be heard when they spoke.

"Lunch will be on in one hour so you can stand up and talk until then," Mama announced before disappearing into the kitchen. I hadn't missed her wiping the tears from her eyes.

Uncle Wade shook my hand, wished me a Happy Birthday and hugged me. He turned to Jake and told him both he and Uncle Rafe expected a visit in the next couple of days. Jake informed them we both had the following two days off and he'd be in touch.

Uncle Rafe didn't bother with a hand shake. He settled for a hug and sloppy kiss, with exaggerated sound, on my cheek.

Steve and Keegan both had their children back in their arms. The little girl appeared shy and she sucked on a thumb, her head against her mother's chest, while eyeing me curiously.

"This is your niece, Liam. Natasha Elizabeth. She's three." Keegan then spoke to her daughter. "This is Uncle Liam. He's been away for a while but he's back now and he's going to visit and play with you and your brother."

I chucked her under the chin and she giggled.

Steve stepped forward, wrapped a hand around my neck and rested his forehead against mine.

"I love you so much, little brother. Welcome back."

The tears threatened to start again.

"Thank you," I whispered.

The little boy squirmed between us and Steve took a step back.

"This is Alexander Liam. His first birthday is today."

"You named him after me?"

"We did."

That got the waterworks started again. I toyed with the little boy's outstretched hand and he giggled and cooed. He was the image of my brother to look at with the same dark hair and vivid blue eyes. Natasha was a mirror image of her mother with the same reddish hair and chocolate brown eyes. They were beautiful children and I looked forward to being an uncle to them both.

Kellie approached me tentatively. She'd disowned me when she'd found out what I'd done. I expected it would be hard for me to be accepted by her.

Without warning, I found her in my arms, sobbing against my shoulder.

"Liam, I'm so sorry. I didn't mean what I said. I was angry. I love you and I've missed you so much."

Erin wrapped her arms around both of us and cried.

"I didn't really hate you. Will you be my brother again?"

I nodded because I couldn't get past the lump in my throat. When Mom and Dad eased the girls away, I turned into Jake's waiting arms.

"Thank you."

"Anything for you, Sweetheart."

Jake pushed me back a few steps, a move that puzzled me until he pulled a small box from his pocket and dropped to one knee. I covered my mouth with both hands and fought back more tears. It was a wonder I hadn't cried myself dry.

"Lee, the first time I saw you, your hair was sticking out in all directions, you were bare chested and bare footed but I knew you were special. In the past four years, I've fallen in love with you a little more every day. I can't imagine my life without you in it. So, Liam Hamish Masters, will you do me the honor of becoming my husband."

I didn't hesitate. I didn't have to think about it. Jake was the half which completed me. "Yes!"

Jake slid a gold band onto the ring finger of my right hand, stood and swept me into his arms. The kiss was deep, seductive. Filled with passion. I'd forgotten about our families and friends, I had eyes for only the man I loved. My face heated when everyone began clapping and whistling. We broke the kiss and I buried my head into Jake's chest. Moments later, we were hugged, kissed and slapped on the back.

"Lunch!" Mama shouted.

We all sat and plate after plate of steaming Italian food was placed on the tables before us. We were seated with our families and I learned, they'd all arrived early so they could chat and get to know each other. I couldn't believe Jake had done all this for me.

"Jake said it's your day off tomorrow, Lee. Will you come and spend some time with us – both of you?" Mom asked.

I glanced at Jake who nodded.

"I'd like that." I turned to Kellie. "Are you in college, Kellie?"

"Yes. I'm in my second year of studying Medicine. I'd like to be a Pediatrician."

"Brains and beauty, huh?"

She giggled at my words.

"What about you, Erin?"

"I'm not sure and I still have a few years of school. I like the idea of working with children, maybe teaching."

"You have plenty of time to decide."

"Mom and Dad said you're a really good dancer. I didn't know you could dance."

I looked across to my parents and Dad explained. "We were there last night with Steve, Keegan and your uncles. Steve visited the club on Friday night when one of his contacts said you were dancing there. He'd been searching for you for a long time. He spoke to Jake and we were invited to come and watch last night."

"You were there, why didn't you ask to see me?"

"Jake was afraid we'd upset you and suggested we meet you here today instead."

"You were wonderful, Liam. I could have watched you all night," Keegan gushed.

"Thank you," I said shyly.

"Jake said you were offered films and stage shows." Dad spoke with pride.

"Yeah, but I'm happy where I am."

"It looks to me like you have everything you need, son."

I glanced at Jake and smiled. "I certainly do, Dad."

The rest of the afternoon was spent chatting with the men from the club, Jake's parents and my family. Mama had made a huge chocolate cake with thick chocolate frosting.

Twenty-one candles decorated the top. I didn't make a wish when I blew them out, I already had more than I could ever wish for. I did give thanks, though. For being reunited with my family, for good friends, Mama and most of all – Jake, the love of my life.

Jake pushed his chair back and patted his knees. I climbed onto his lap and his arms closed around me. I rested my head on his shoulder and listened to him talking with Dad. I drifted into thought, recalling the four years since I'd left home.

I'd come a long way and finally believed, I could forgive myself for what had happened. I'd never stopped loving my family and to have them back in my life, to be given a second chance, was something I'd always be grateful to Jake for. I dreaded thinking where I might have ended up if I hadn't met him.

I'd been born wild. Strong-willed. Defiant. And, as every day had passed, became more jealous of my brother. The pieces had finally slotted together. I was whole. Engaged to a man I loved and adored. I was finally at peace with myself. We had our entire lives before us.

"You look tired, son. You had a late night last night." Mom brushed stray hairs from my forehead.

"It's all been overwhelming, Mom and I am tired, but happy."

"Take him home, Jake and we'll see you tomorrow." Mom kissed my cheek before leaning over and placing a kiss to Jake's cheek.

We both stood and Jake encased my hand in his. It took us almost half an hour to thank everyone and say goodnight. Roan had his car and offered to deliver my gifts to our apartment the following day.

When we stepped outside, the cool air wrapped around us. Jake turned me into his embrace and kissed me deeply. When we parted, I reached up and cupped his cheek with my hand.

"I love you so very much. Thank you, Jake. You gave me my life, my family and your love. It's the best birthday I've ever had."

"I believe we have some unfinished business, Sweetheart."

"We certainly do."

Laughing, we turned and headed for home.

The day had been perfect.

Life was perfect.

## About the Author

I write romance from sweet to hot.

Strong social themes are a feature in my books.

I grew up in Manly, NSW, Australia, and have traveled Australia and the World on postings with my Naval Officer husband of 48 years.

I live with my husband and fur baby–Gemma-Jean, a young Jack Russell Terrier, in a small village in the mountains in Queensland, Australia.

Since retiring from a nursing career of 37 years, I have been able to indulge my passion for writing.

Our family enjoys traveling the country with our RV when not at home renovating.

# Author Links

Newsletter:
http://eepurl.com/hyPb5L

SUSAN HORSNELL
Linktree
https://linktr.ee/SusanHorsnell

SUSAN R. HORSNELL
Linktree:
https://linktr.ee/SusanRHorsnell

Ingram Content Group UK Ltd.
Milton Keynes UK
UKHW020700240723
425668UK00014B/626